THE SCANDALOUS MISADVENTURES OF HIRAM GRANGE
BOOK 5

HIRAM GRANGE

&

the Nymphs of Krakow

by

Richard Wright

SHROUD PUBLISHING
MILTON, NH

Richard Wright

HIRAM GRANGE
& the Nymphs of Krakow

from
Shroud Publishing

You are holding a limited edition small press novella in your hands.
This book is a result of hard work and creative effort.
Enjoy it, and celebrate the possibility of all things.

First Edition

First Printing July 2010
Copyright © 2010 Shroud Publishing
All Rights Reserved

Editor: Tim Deal
Cover & Interior Paintings by Malcolm McClinton
Book Design, Copy-editing & Illustrations by Danny Evarts

The text of this book was composed using Adobe Garamond Pro.
Display type was set in Cracked and Charlemagne Std.

ISBN: 978-0-9827275-1-5

Shroud Publishing LLC
121 Mason Road
Milton, NH 03851
www.shroudmagazine.com

~DEDICATION~

*For my wife Kirsty, who probably didn't realise
her birthday jaunt to Krakow was a research trip in disguise,
and my daughter Eva, who makes me cards with
monsters on for inspiration.*

---

*For Tim Deal, Hiram's daddy, who let me play
with his monstrous offspring.*

---

*For Jake, Scott, Rob, Kevin, Malcolm, and Danny,
for advice, suggestions, inspiration, and more.*

HIRAM GRANGE

&
the Nymphs of Krakow

Hiram

slammed through the door into the cinema bar, whipping it shut on the corridor behind him. Something heavy hit hard from the other side, staggering him forward, and he threw his weight back, sneering through the fear as he forced it flush. Door closed, legs straining as he struggled to stop his feet slipping beneath the vast strength trying to knock him aside, he scanned the room. No staff, no customers, just bottles and bottles of sweet beers and spirits, calling him over.

"Later, my dears," he told them through gritted teeth. "I'm a tad busy."

It should have been such a simple kill. A name, a place, a little background—more than he was often given when Mrs Bothwell issued his assignments. His current predicament was of his own design, bred of complacency and distraction. The Man in the Bad Hat had even tried warning him, but to no avail. Hiram had struggled to focus on the task in hand, and it was all the fault of that bitch, Kedra. After dogging his tracks for months, a lean shadow who had hauled his wiry arse out of more than one fire unasked, she had finally chosen to step into the light. At first she had entranced him. Her square shoulders and lean body, small firm breasts perfect beneath leather, were a scarred reminder of his one true love, Jodie. While the actress had yet to recognise her feelings for him, he had dallied with the notion that this woman, Gabrysia Kedra, could satisfy him in her absence.

Within minutes she had torn his world apart with elaborate fantasies of secret organisations and hierarchies. Lies and fabrications, clearly wrought to unnerve and unbalance him, but to what end?

The thing on the other side of the door pushed again, and he cried out, his strength fading fast. Even now she distracted him, and he needed to focus, to devise a solution. It was massive, many times stronger than he was. Simple physics told him he was going to lose this inverted tug of war. Sweat dripped down his roman nose. There was one exit from the bar, and he was wrestling to keep that shut. He couldn't see a fire door. He would remember to discuss that with the health and safety people, should he meet them in the afterlife. The windows looked like reinforced glass, and he was four storeys up.

A flimsy panel of wood away, the thing screeched in frustration. The sound, impossibly shrill, pierced him like a sharp and tearing blade. He collapsed to the floor, doubling up as something delicate ruptured inside him. Bottles shattered along the bar like they were being raked with automatic fire, casting glass and fluids of all colours and tastes across the room. The windows blew outwards with an elegance worthy of slow motion. Scarlet warmth burst from his ears and nose.

A werebat. Of all the bloody things to expect. When Hiram first saw it in front of the cinema screen, first heard it tear the air in two, he had silently applauded the movie's special effects team, even as he dropped his Webley, tooled up with silver bullets, in order to clutch his ears. He had last seen the gun sliding beneath a bank of seats, as he cursed Bothwell for her lack of specificity. *Lycanthrope*, she told him. Of course he had assumed it would be a wolf.

It gave a final push.

He was still on the floor, prone, unable to stop the door from opening.

It stepped into the bar, the stench of wet fur and death rolling ahead of it.

The windows were blown out.

He was on the fourth floor.

A muscular flex of wings, an impression of hair and teeth above him.

Pushing himself to his feet, Hiram bolted. Claws raked the back of his suit jacket as he went, slicing skin and drawing a scream from him. His foot hit the window edge, glass shards penetrating his sole.

Four storeys up, Hiram erupted into the night sky, the sense of space, of void, crushing his sense of self, and he prayed to whatever gods might still consider his worth.

And a dark and shrieking winged thing followed close behind.

Mrs Bothwell waited politely for the still-screaming cinema audience to trample one another onto the street, wondering how much they had seen in the gloom of the auditorium. Hiram had been fast, arresting the beast's attention before it could decide on a victim, drawing it away. She doubted that any two witnesses would give the same story to the authorities, if any of them could manage a coherent account at all, and that suited her to perfection. Reliable witnesses would need to be attended to carefully, for fear of setting panic free in the streets. Her people called it containment. The world was not ready to know of the shadow things that flitted in and out of it, or the struggles that waged on the edge of a reality far more fragile than most of mankind could comprehend.

She patted her trim, practical handbag, feeling Hiram's precious Webley nestled amongst her tissues. She had watched him lose the weapon with pursed lips. The opportunity to see him in action was a rare thing—it was her job to point him towards danger, not trot along after like some eager cheerleader—and she had to confess that deep down she was disappointed. How he intended to dispatch this foe without the silver bullets he had managed to acquire was beyond her. Despite her doubts, he would likely find a way. Improvisation was one of his great gifts, and had made him the longest-lived agent she had recruited. Caleb had been the shortest, she remembered. Two weeks. Barely time to learn how to point and shoot. Her superiors had not been impressed with his under-performance, or hers as his handler, and for a while she had believed that they might be considering her expendability. Then she found Hiram, and her status improved. No wonder she was fond of him.

An elbow caught her between the ribs, a straggler putting his own safety before that of this thin, prim old lady before him. No manners at all. She flicked her wrist, rotating the umbrella in her hand one hundred and eighty degrees, where the reinforced tip crashed into his temple with force enough to drop him like a sack of potatoes. The man, a bruiser at six feet with a boxer's build, hit the floor and lay there twitching, a low groan drooling from his lips. Lesson learned. Courtesy cost nothing.

Behind her, three bewildered members of staff watched warily, too confused by the stampede to raise a challenge. She gave a matronly smile and left them to their anxious bemusement. However Hiram intended to finish the job, he would not risk bringing the creature back through the multiplex, so it was safe enough to leave them where they were and wait for him in the street.

She stepped onto the sidewalk, heaving with previously desperate escapees who now decided to fulfil the role of idiot crowd, and heard glass shatter above her head. The mentally deficient around her looked up, as though the situation really merited a detailed assessment. Mrs Bothwell popped open her umbrella and raised it above her head. A second later the thud and patter of broken glass vibrated through her canopy, as the rest of the crowd were showered with tiny, slicing shards of pain.

More screaming and aimless running, away from her this time, and she saw blood dripping from fresh wounds. It all looked superficial enough, and with luck would be sufficient to encourage the herd out of the general area. With the last of the glass pattering at her feet, she closed the brolly and looked up. Hiram was dropping towards her like a stone, arms outstretched as though they could slow his descent. The bat plummeted after, wings drawn in as it bared the dozens of teeth in its wrinkled, mortar-shell maw. She raised her eyebrows and stepped back, certain they would crash right into her. As the werebat caught up to Hiram, barely ten feet above her, it extended its wings with a crack, arresting its descent as it snapped at its prey.

Hiram caught her eye, and there was a second of recognition and surprise on his narrow face.

Then he twisted, throwing his arms around the werebat's neck and flipping his legs around its waist. The creature shrieked, bore down with those great wings, and drove them back into the sky.

Mrs Bothwell stared, the wind from the down thrust flattening her hair. If she had reached out, she could almost have touched them. They gained erratic height, the bat frantically trying to scratch away its new passenger, people in the street following the progress of the struggling duo. With a sigh, she pulled her phone from her bag.

There were going to be some containment issues after all.

As the city span around him, a bewildering kaleidoscope of lights, Hiram hung on to the creature's neck for dear life, pulling himself cheek to cheek to avoid its massive, drooling maw. One bite was all it would take to consign him to a winged future amidst the spires and towers of the city—flapping, and screaming, and killing.

Since seizing the creature, he had lost his sense of direction, and knew only that they were rising fast. It shrieked, and the noise jabbed down his spine. His legs jerked in response, but he held tight, feeling the muscles beneath the foul-smelling fur roil as it struggled to keep them both aloft. Sudden winds slapped him, and while he couldn't risk a glance, he guessed that they had cleared the height of the building.

Claws raked his side, ripping up flesh along his ribs, and he gave a shriek of his own, pitiful and human next to the bat's brain-freezing cries. This couldn't go on forever. Soon enough, the bat would realise that it had only to put down on the nearest brownstone, and it could tear him apart at its leisure. He needed a plan.

He didn't have one, and so settled on changing the dynamic a little, hoping that new opportunities might present themselves. Hugging the bat to him with his left arm, he flicked his right out to one side. As the knife shot forth from the forearm sheath he had worn since the horrors in London, he had a moment of panic, believing absolutely that he had misjudged the timing and his last remaining weapon was plummeting to the street below. When his fingers closed around the handle, he relaxed more than should have been possible, so far above the world. He drew back, feeling the bat tense in anticipation of a clear bite at his face. It was grinning.

Hiram grinned back, and slid his knife into its right eye.

It spasmed with immense force, and his legs lost purchase on the creature's waist. He slipped free, heart pounding for the weightless moment before he caught himself on a wet fistful of fur at its neck, letting his own momentum swing him around until he could grasp the handle of the embedded blade with his other hand. The bat snapped feebly at his face, and rank drool splattered his chin, the smell of rotten meat diving into his nostrils as they thrashed in the air. He glimpsed the street as they tumbled, horribly close, traffic stopped as faces peered up. He wondered if his audience could see his stomach, which he could only imagine was somewhere far above, following him towards a two-dimensional end.

He calculated his chances of survival. It wasn't complex math.

The bat's wings stiffened, and their plummet slowed so abruptly that he almost lost his grip again. The drop snapped into a fast, shallow glide along the street. They shot above the traffic, the bat still dazed as they dipped down, weaving between the vehicles, and then Hiram's dangling heels smacked the road, bouncing up, then smacking down one more time, hard enough

to drag him from his nemesis, crashing him to the tarmac. Momentum skidded him further, and he rolled to gain some control. A rib snapped, popping dully inside him, blooming fire through his insides.

At last he stopped, sprawled on the road, hardly able to convince his body that it really had ceased rolling, sliding, and falling. He longed for the luxurious embrace of unconsciousness. An ambulance would complete the picture perfectly. There would be drugs in an ambulance. An ambulance crew, too, but therein lay the problem. Where ambulance crews appeared, police officers often followed, and he couldn't be around when they arrived. Sitting up, hissing as his broken rib stabbed him, he shook his head to clear his doubled vision. There were people gathering, their faces gaining definition as his eyes found focus. Some were concerned, but others were curious, and these worried him. Curious people intervened.

"You okay, buddy?" The question came from an overweight Caucasian in a rumpled suit. There was lipstick on his collar, and Hiram wondered if it had been put there by a wife or a mistress.

"Where did it go?"

"Where did what go?"

Hiram took a steadying breath and stood, his left leg barely able to take weight. "Surely you aren't mocking me, sir?" Regardless of how torn and bloodied he felt, or perhaps because that was the precise picture he presented, the man stepped back, his face a little whiter than before, and nodded along the street.

Hiram saw it, thirty metres on. It had slammed into the side of a vacated yellow taxi, crumpling the door, and lay prone on the ground, neck twisted at so sharp an angle that a sympathetic shudder went down Hiram's back. The involuntary movement was enough to buckle his weak leg, and he went down on one knee, teeth clenched as little explosions of pain popped his hip. The recovery time from this little skirmish was something he looked forward to very much. His pipe would be close to hand, as would the green fairy, Mistress Absinthe. And girls. He would find girls, and make them wear uniforms.

"Buddy?"

Hiram ignored the distant voice as the world greyed along the edges of his vision.

"Buddy, it's still kicking. You hear me? I just saw it move."

"You kill it then." Why were the sheep always so willing to step back and let him save them? The bat was crippled, barely conscious, and still they waited for him to dispatch it. He took a deep breath, coughing it back out and tasting blood in his throat. Weary beyond words, he saw the bat jerk its head, trying to realign its spine. The movement was feeble, but would soon grow in strength. Only one thing could put down a lycanthrope with any permanence. Trapping a whimper in his own throat, aware of the growing audience, he pushed to his feet, rocking on his heels for a second before stumbling forwards. Momentum and gravity kept him moving, despite the objections of the flesh.

The bat growled deep in its throat as he reached it, a quiver running along one outstretched wing as it scented his presence. Hiram flicked his wrist, then stared at empty fingers, wondering where his knife was. "Ah yes," he said, feeling giddy and strange, "my apologies, viewers." Leaning down, he grabbed the handle of his knife, still embedded in the bat's eye. Giving a brutal twist of the blade to reopen the already healing wound, he jerked it free. The bat arched its back, wings flexing feebly as Hiram pulled his keys from his pocket. Struggling to focus, he pinched off the silver *I Love Belfast* fob he had picked up in Northern Ireland. It was supposed to be a fairy, but looked more like a Leprechaun, which was why he liked it. He hated Faeries.

The bat sensed the proximity of the metal, and tensed for a final bid at freedom.

Hiram leaned forward and dropped the fob into the bat's moist, gaping eye socket, and the beast stilled as the silver did its instant work.

Hiram smiled, then frowned when he couldn't straighten up. He heard far-off sirens wailing, but his body's insistence that everything stop, immediately, rolled over him, and he collapsed across his prey, dead to the world.

"**H**e looks so weak, lying there."

"Your opinion was not invited."

"Are you certain he can do this?"

"Why? Are you volunteering to take his place?"

"Of course not."

"Then close your mouth and get him in the car. The police are almost here."

"As you wish."

"Gently. You're going to fix him up. That doesn't mean you can break him first."

"He needs more than field treatment."

"It's all he's getting. Make it count."

Hiram woke slowly, a baby stumbling through thick fog. At first, he couldn't remember who he was, but this was not an unfamiliar sensation, and a moment later it came to him. Hiram Grange. Defender of the natural order, preserver of the status quo. To which he added, a second after the pains running up the left side of his body hit him, punching bag for the supernatural.

There were drugs in his system, none of them his preferred varieties, but they were dulling the sharp bite of his injuries, so he supposed he should be grateful. Eyes closed, he heard the purr of an engine, felt a vehicle rock beneath him. Squad car? Ambulance? Neither were a positive development, for they suggested there would soon be questions posed that he would rather not answer. He tensed, preparing to make his escape. Once they realised he was awake, there would be scant seconds in which to act, and somebody would probably get hurt. This was fine, as long as it wasn't him. The greater good, and all that.

Snapping his eyes open, he sat bolt upright, gritting his teeth against the wave of broken-glass nausea that chased him. Mrs Bothwell, sitting beside him in the back of the limousine, tinted windows muting the city lights behind her, scarcely flinched. There was a glass in her hand, and his finely tuned nose detected the mellow hint of aged whisky. "For medicinal purposes," she said, holding it out. "Don't gulp it." He stared at her a moment, wondering what she was doing there. When he glimpsed her during his fall, he had been certain he was mistaken. Bothwell left the fieldwork to him. While he had never been certain what other resources his eccentric sponsor could draw on in her singular campaign against the dark forces, he knew that he was her final solution, a blunt weapon to be used against the horrors teeming along the edges of the mundane. Having her turn up in the field felt strange and intrusive.

"What are you doing here?"

"In a moment. Sip the whisky."

Ignoring her advice on consumptive etiquette, he took the glass and knocked it back in one. Not bad, though a little water would have opened up the flavour. Then it hit his stomach, and he closed his eyes while the urge to vomit passed. "What have you given me?"

"I don't know. Alphonse?" Hiram gritted his teeth. Of course her driver was there. The man's voice, cold and clinical, turned Hiram's stomach again.

"A cocktail of my own devising. It will wear off around the time you disembark the plane."

"You have a broken rib and significant bruising on your left side," Bothwell broke in. "When the drugs wear off, it's going to hurt."

Hiram felt the bandages wrapped around his torso, only then noticing that somebody had changed his suit. "I don't recall bringing a change of clothes."

"We stopped to pack you a case."

"You broke into my Airstream?"

"Your defences are less formidable than you imagine."

"You have many pretty things," Alphonse said, the lack of inflection making it hard for Hiram to judge whether he was being mocked. Erring on the side of probability, he was about to snap back a rejoinder when his brain caught up with the discussion.

"What plane? There's a plane?"

"There is an urgent matter," said Bothwell, watching him closely. "It requires your subtle touch." Now he really was being mocked, and her scorn cut him more than he cared to admit. "A situation has come to our attention in Krakow." One of the biggest confluences, though Hiram had never been tasked there. Uniquely, the Krakow confluence had a back door, a rip in the world opened nearly seventy years ago at Auschwitz. Reality had borne the intensity of death and degradation there poorly.

Something else tickled his mind, something about Poland, but he couldn't put his finger on it. "Unless the city is being held in the grip of terror by a marauding three-year-old, I'm in no condition to deal with it."

Bothwell raised an eyebrow. "Really? Shall we ask the ancient evil to stand down until you're recovered?"

Hiram's face flushed. "What's the kill?"

"That's better. You're tracking a rusalka, a creature formed of the spirit of a murdered woman or girl. Normally they're pests, lurking along riverbanks in Russia and Eastern Europe, seducing men to their watery deaths, occasionally taking a more aggressive approach to their vengeance. This one is different. It has an agenda, and is prepared to travel the world to achieve it. Indeed, it has already done so."

The limo went over a pothole, and a wave of pain splashed up his side as it bounced. "What agenda?" he asked, through gritted teeth.

"The creature has targeted me."

Surprise made Hiram forget his woes. "Impossible."

"I would have thought so, yet three of my contacts in Europe have been executed. Its tactics go beyond assassination, however. They extend to disinformation and sabotage."

Hiram considered. Since he had joined Bothwell's cause as her pet killer, he had never known her to be attacked directly. She stayed in the shadows to avoid that very scenario, but he supposed the situation was inevitable. Things were serious indeed.

"How do I find it?"

"I doubt that will be difficult. I have no idea how it is sourcing its information, but I suspect it will not be long before it becomes aware of your arrival in its home territory. All you need do is draw it out."

He grunted, seeing the subtext. "I'm bait."

"Yes."

"This thing, your rusalka, passes for human?" She nodded. "You have a photo?"

"No. I didn't imagine you would need one."

"Really? I'm to go to Poland and wait for a woman I don't know to try to kill me?"

"Hardly. You'll know her when you see her. You've met her before." Hiram closed his eyes as he realised why the mention of Poland had given him pause. "She uses the name Gabrysia Kedra when she tries to turn my allies against me. I can't tell you how disappointed I am that you failed to mention your encounters with her."

The in-flight movie was disappointing. Hiram had thought that one of Jodie's films might be listed. Perhaps the family-friendly piece of fluff, set on a desert island, that he had not yet seen. It would give her opportunity to expose her flesh to him. If she could, then he knew she would, though now he would have to wait for a more private occasion to find out. It was for the best. Squeezed into the centre of the row of seats, between the obese, sweating lady to his left, whose concept of comfortable clothing appeared to stray no further than the Adidas brand, and the garlic-scented boy in the window seat on his right, the arousal Jodie would stir in him would be impossible to attend to without causing a major airborne incident.

The woman shifted, her flabby elbow flopping against his ribs, and he hissed. She turned in surprise, blotchy chins wobbling. "An injury," he said. "I would appreciate a little care." She nodded, taking in the paleness of his skin, the pain lining his eyes, and fixed her attention back on Will Smith's screen hijinks with fresh resolve. They had been in the air for several hours, enough time for Hiram to have collected a number of empty bottles on the tray in front of him. Alphonse's painkiller cocktail was wearing off, and deep, sore canyons inside him were widening by the hour. The airline's cheap, blended whisky helped him float above those depths a little longer, but he was reluctant to indulge too wantonly without knowing exactly what Bothwell's driver had shot him full of. Even his personal abuse of opiates was based on knowledge and experience, his addictions tempered by the illusion of self-control. Since Sadie's death, he had accepted that it had to be thus. The consequences were too much to bear when he let himself stray while on the hunt. His line of work demanded that he remain able to select the moments of his most hideous indulgence, slotting them between professional engagements rather than remaining their full-time slave.

His line of work. Since Bothwell had dropped him off at the airport, thrusting tickets into his hand, he had avoided thinking on that very issue. To do so forced him to consider Gabrysia Kedra, his shadow over the past two years, his guardian angel when he most needed one, exposing herself only to assist him in the direst circumstances. In Great Bay, she had been watching as the dead rose and he put them back down. When Hitler returned, time and again, she had observed Hiram's folly, and the final price of his addictions. In Boston, she had shoved a needle into his heart, the adrenaline saving his life, freeing him to pursue Giblis. In Northern Ireland he had believed he was beyond her reach, finally, but after Mab and Therese there was London, and his face-off with the thing that had once been a man called the Ripper. After saving him from plummeting to his death, she spoke to him, offering a bizarre story, attempting to undermine his understanding of his own role in the world.

Mrs Bothwell, she had insisted, was not the eccentric crusader against dark forces that he thought her to be, did not build her small team of operatives, with Hiram at the fore, alone. There were other forces pulling the strings, other teams just like his, all operating under the cover of OIRA, the Office of Independent Research & Analysis. Bothwell was just another lowly grunt like him.

The notion appalled him, flew in the face of everything he knew to be true, and he had driven Kedra away in a most ungracious fashion. To accept her story was to embrace his history, his reason for waking each morning, as a lie. It would require staggering levels of deceit from Bothwell, dating back through the years since she had found him, broken and alone. Worse still, Kedra's story required him to believe that he was not unique. There would have to be others like him, and he could not swallow the idea, was unwilling even to consider the possibility. That Kedra could be one such … no. The Office was a clever cover devised by Mrs Bothwell, a crusader who had drawn her team together using her own wealth and resources. She had found Hiram when she most needed him. Only Hiram had the combination of qualities, forged in the trauma of his mother's insanity and suicide, his father's brash religion, that Bothwell needed to front her team.

Only Hiram, because he was special. He had to be, or everything he had suffered was meaningless chance, random cruelty.

All of this battled in his mind as Kedra spoke, until he erupted in scorn and fury, casting her from him like some biblical demon. How she even knew of Bothwell and The Office was beyond his comprehension, and perhaps he had been foolish not to report the encounter, but he had been baffled, even unnerved. Nothing unnerved Hiram Grange, and admitting to this rare exception had driven him to a binge of absinthe and cruelty-fuelled sex that had exhausted his local supply of willing young goths. Emerging from this period of self-prescribed therapy, he continued to be haunted by Kedra's bizarre theories. They cut at his sense of purpose, eroding his focus.

To discover that he had been played was a guilty relief, even if her motives were unclear. Why was she going after Bothwell? Was there a history there that he was not privy to? Was Bothwell withholding information?

Troubled, in more than a little pain, he latched his seat belt as the sign above his head lit up, and the plane descended towards Poland.

As far as Hiram could tell, the driver waiting for him at the John Paul II International airport was locally engaged, and had no idea of his true identity and purpose. The swarthy young man brandished a handwritten sign reading *Harry Kranj*, and Hiram limped past it three times before realising that it was a mangled version of his own name. His cover as an auditor for the International Consortium of Universities, evaluating University-funded research the world over, was in his real name, and he rarely used an alias. This error spoke clearly of the rush with which the assignment had been thrown together, making him even more uneasy.

So, too, did the fact that the driver was not part of Bothwell's extended network of associates. Often he would be met on landing in a new part of the world by an ally who would speed him on his way to whatever kill was required. Was it possible that everybody Bothwell knew in Poland had been sought out and crushed by this rusalka? The presence of a major confluence at the heart of Krakow, waiting for something to punch through from the strange, dark places on the far side, guaranteed that she would have cultivated contacts in the city. She had mentioned that some of her allies had been eliminated already, and the implications of that statement started to hit home.

The driver didn't introduce himself as he carried Hiram's bag through the airport, and he wondered if all Poles were so surly and guarded. The airport itself still wore the telltale costume of previous eras, before the nation fled Russia's embrace to find a cautious welcome as part of the European Union. The immigration staff greeting him were uniformed soldiers, and military vehicles dotted the runways.

The driver pulled away, weaving the car along small, winding country roads as evening drew in. Hiram saw horses tethered to ruined old cars, pulling them along as makeshift wagons. Houses crumbled into the land, and there was a grimness to the people they passed, poverty wrapping them up and dimming them. His young driver refrained from the usual small talk usually reserved for such brief journeys, failing entirely to tout the best tourist attractions and brothels.

When they reached Krakow, the country's personality changed. They passed bars and coffeehouses, flourishing restaurants and ornate gothic churches. The city, to his relief, was full of life, flourishing on the tourist dollar that had followed its leap into the western world. Almost untouched by the World Wars, the medieval streets were redolent with age, a bustling jumble of unspoiled antiquity. There were churches everywhere. This city had birthed a pope, and wore Catholicism with fierce pride. Hiram knew from experience that faiths grew strong in the shadow of a confluence; a primitive, primal reaction to the evils that festered in the belly of such places. Yet while the natives wrapped themselves in God and cowered, not so the many visitors. A vomiting stag party, propping themselves outside a bar as the locals glowered, set the tone as they neared the city centre.

Finally, the driver pulled up on a long street with high kerbs, next to a large, arched wooden doorway that would lead to his apartment. Hiram's pain and nausea were cresting dizzying new heights. Not only had the painkillers worn off, but dehydration from his bottled indulgence on the plane also wracked him. His flesh felt like refrigerated clay as he stepped from the back of the car, and he stumbled when his left leg tried to take his weight. The driver took his case to the door. "Rynek Glowny is round the corner," he said, placing a key in the lock of the regular door set into the archway. "Big square. Very old, very pretty. Many restaurants, much drinking." Hiram smiled. Much drinking sounded very promising indeed. "I take your bag?"

"Please do." Unsure whether he could even get the case inside on his own, he wondered how he was supposed to carry out this assignment in his current state. Could this rusalka thing not have waited another week for his attention? As the driver pushed the door inwards, Hiram followed, dusting a few flakes of snow from his shoulders. The weather was taking a turn for the worse, and he hoped privately for blizzards so severe that he would be stuck indoors for days.

Inside was a large, paved chamber. Given the arched doors behind him, he assumed the whole building had once been an inn of some sort, and this the entrance for coaches and horses. Doors on either side led to ground floor apartments, but they would not be his. Bothwell never put him on the ground floor. It was too vulnerable a position, if he were to be attacked. Of course, many of the things that were wont to attack him gave no consideration to traditional entrances and exits, but the precaution was sound, and he nodded as the driver led him up a wide, smooth-stepped stairway. Limping badly, letting the cast iron banister take much of his weight, he followed to the first floor. The stairs continued upwards, but the driver stopped on the long landing. There were three black painted doors, and the driver led him to the last, at the back of the building, exactly where Hiram would have chosen if booking it himself. Potential escape routes to the ground and upper floors, set away from the building frontage, with thick, solid doors. It was defensible, and earned his appreciation.

The driver unlocked the door, pushing it open to reveal a narrow, softly lit hallway leading left to a clean, high-ceilinged sitting room with huge windows overlooking an alley. A small kitchen sat to one side of the room, and above it a platform, accessed by ladder, held the bed, giving the kitchen itself an artificially low ceiling. Next to the window, on a table by the couch, sat a small parcel, a bottle of absinthe, and a sealed envelope.

Dropping Hiram's case by the couch, glancing nervously around, the driver offered him the keys to the apartment. "You have tip?"

Hiram palmed the keys. "Certainly. Consider being more gregarious." The driver's English clearly didn't stretch so far but, after giving Hiram a sullen stare good enough to be patented, he appeared to get the message.

"*Baba z wozu!*" The driver marched out, slamming the door, and Hiram heard the tumblers roll. At least the oaf had the courtesy to lock the door.

Left alone, Hiram found the lure of the bed above impossibly strong, but that was countered in part by the verdant pull of the absinthe. Torn between the two, unable to decide, he instead tore at the parcel with weary hands, popping a flap open. Inside, as expected, was his Webley break-top and a box of cartridges. Tucked in with them was a small jar of pills. It amazed him, as ever, that his gun, in Mrs Bothwell's possession when she dropped him at the airport, had somehow reached Poland before him. Once upon a time, he had believed that the waiting weapons must be different guns, sourced perhaps for their similarity, but he knew his own Webley, even before checking for the one spent shell that had killed his mother, the one he would never replace though it left him only five shots per load. To be certain, he had once made three tiny scratches around the barrel of the pistol before handing it over in America. Sure enough, those tiny marks were there when he was passed the gun at São Paulo. Since then, he had learned to trust Bothwell, and the shame at doubting her on the word of this rusalka thing became more pronounced as he loaded five fresh rounds and closed the weapon.

The weight was slightly off, and he checked one of the spare shells from the box to find out why. The bullet clutched in the rimmed cartridge was silver and iron-laced, which meant that Bothwell's armourers were not entirely sure what would be required to put the creature he hunted in the ground. Iron was probably the right way to go, his guess being that a physically embodied wraith would have more in common with the Faerie than anything else, but a little silver was never a bad idea. Satisfied, he slipped a fistful of extra rounds into his trouser pocket, and rested the Webley on the table while he examined the pills. A handwritten label read: *Your loyal servant, Alphonse.* The writing was tidy and annoying, like the master of the hand that wrote it, somehow conveying worlds of contempt through four brief words. Still, the painkillers had been effective in America, so he popped the cap and liberated a couple of the small blue pills. Eyeing the absinthe, he decided not to waste it on medicinal purposes, instead shuffling into the kitchen, finding a glass in the cupboard above the sink and filling it from the tap.

Washing the pills down, feeling a little better just at the thought that the pain might soon mute, he found the bathroom off the hallway and stripped to the waist. The full-length mirror behind the door showed a hollow-eyed wreck of a man, his ribs and narrow waist an exotic blending of blacks and purples, his hair lank and bedraggled. After the flight, he really needed a shower, but the thought of re-strapping his torso afterwards dissuaded him, and he instead filled the sink with hot water to wash himself down. Taking care not to soak the bandages, he turned his thoughts to the rusalka and how to drive it into the open. Bothwell's suggestion that he sit around and wait for it to notice him, well-meaning though it was, lacked appeal. Hiram preferred a *carpe diem* approach to his assignments.

What little he already knew about the creature came from occasional references in his studies of mythology and cryptozoology. Bothwell had confirmed that it was a water spirit, which meant the tie to moving bodies of water should be strong. The Kedra rusalka must be powerful, to travel so far from the well of its power, but it would still have to return to replenish itself, if it had not already. Krakow sat on the Vistula river, which would be his first port of call. If he achieved nothing more than attracting its attention sooner rather than later, it would not be a wasted effort. Beaten and wretched as he felt, he craved home comforts, and wanted this venture done with.

Drying off, feeling a little refreshed, he went back to the sitting room and opened his case. Slipping on a fresh shirt, he stood at the window as he buttoned it up. He wasn't sure whether the building on the other side of the alley was actually a church, but the three half-size alabaster saints recessed into the first floor wall strongly suggested as much. The alley was narrow, less than two car widths across. Snow fell heavily, burying the cobbles below, and he felt the Polish chill radiating from the glass. Not ideal weather for wraith-hunting, though if he were in more robust health he would have tried it anyway.

Having convinced himself that he would stay in the apartment for at least this one night, he approached the bottled Green Fairy, recognising the brand and studying it respectfully. It was *Apsinthion*, a Polish absinthe made and bottled by hand according to an eighteenth-century Swiss recipe. While he had heard of it, the opportunity to sample had never presented itself. Bothwell had admirable taste, though the gift was an unusual gesture. She rarely passed meaningful comment on his off-duty entertainments, but he was certain she would not wish to encourage indulgence while on the job. That would hardly stop him from doing as he chose, for he deemed himself a fairer judge of when his addictions were becoming impediments than had once been the case, but her new role as provider sat uncomfortably. Perhaps she felt guilty for breaking into his Airstream. If so, she need not have troubled herself. While his pride had been wounded at the inadequacy of his defences, her breach of them was a lesson learned. Opening the bottle, he took a deep sniff, letting the bitterness roll over his palate, surprised at the depth of sweetness that followed. Already, he felt his muscles unclenching, and he took the bottle to the kitchen and his waiting glass. A blend this fine needed to be savoured in the traditional way, with ice water dripped into it through sugar, but his brief search of the cupboards revealed no such provisions.

Pursing his lips, he put the bottle down. After the exertions of the previous thirty hours, he deserved to enjoy this properly, and it made his palms sweaty just knowing his own absinthe spoons were in his trailer on the other side of the world. Forgoing the sugar too was inconceivable. He had seen a store a few doors down from his building, and it would take him only a few minutes to get there, pick up some sugar cubes, and return. Opposite the store had been what appeared to be a nightclub or bar, and he was certain he would also be able to procure some narcotic relief to pile atop the pharmaceutical brew already lifting him from the pain's jagged surface. Yanking a heavy trench coat from his bag, he slipped it on, dropping the Webley into one deep pocket. Braced for the cold, pleased that his limp was less pronounced than before, he walked to the door.

Pulling the handle, he found it locked, and remembered the tumblers clicking as the driver stormed out. He dug out his keys, made to insert them in the lock, and stopped. A metal plate had been screwed over the keyhole, the screw heads carefully melted down to prevent them from being removed.

The driver had locked the door. Yet the driver had handed him the keys before leaving. How had he locked the door?

Cursing himself for an idiot, Hiram dropped the useless keys, wondering what they were really for, and dashed back to the sitting room. Snatching up the envelope, ripping it open, he stared at the short, pointed note inside.

Your very brief health, the note read, in chaotic, spiky handwriting a world away from Bothwell's mannered calligraphy. The paper was scented with lilac. Hurling it aside, he scrutinised the room, licking the sudden sweat from his thick lips. There was nothing out of place around the furniture, nothing in the kitchen units or the bathroom. That left the bed on its high platform, and now that he knew what to look for he saw how it sat awkwardly, as though it had been lifted up and placed carelessly back down. Somebody had planted something under the bed.

He had no idea how long he had, or why he was still alive to ask the question, but he had to get out. The door was no longer an option. The windows, he knew without checking, would also be sealed tight, but they remained his only chance. Rushing to the kitchen, he jerked the microwave's plug from its socket, lifting the unit from the counter and running back to the window. Swinging it once, he let fly, grunting with satisfaction as it crashed through glass and wood. Icy winds blew snow through the jagged gap, and he heard the microwave shatter on the street below.

Above him, beneath the bed, something started beeping. The bitch had wired the window, his only exit, as the trigger. Sprinting forward, out of time, he leaped, tucking his knees and head to his chest and half turning in the air so that his back and shoulders knocked free the glass that remained in the frame as he passed through.

He was barely on the street side of the window when the apartment exploded, the fireball catching him in the face and shoving him with cruel force at the opposite wall with a deafening, super-hot growl. Saint Paul, magnificent in alabaster, greeted him, arms outstretched.

Burned by the receding fires, achingly tired of being tossed about above city streets, Hiram clung to the statue as debris rained down on the cobbles below.

"Have you heard from him?"

"Nothing since he boarded the aircraft. His gun never reached the hotel room we had ready for him. Our driver is missing. We presume she will remain so."

"The bitch is good."

"Of course she is. You would be disappointed if it were otherwise."

"He is also supposed to be good, is that not so? Or have you done less well with him than you believed?"

"He was almost crippled in New York. You knew he was not ready. You insisted we dispatch him anyway."

"Actions based on your faith in him over the years. Perhaps your objectivity has become marred. He has survived much, for one of yours. Long enough to develop a fondness for?"

"You blame me for the situation with the woman?"

"No. You know who was responsible for that. I can hardly reach into the Abyss to make an example of him though, can I?"

"Really?"

"Perhaps I could, but a more visible local deterrent may be required. Do we assume she has taken him out of play? Do we engage the third?"

"A moment. There has been a report. I ... yes. An explosion, near the Rynek Glowny. It could be him."

"Then the third stays silent. They cannot cross paths. Until we confirm otherwise, we consider Grange to be in play."

"Very well."

"If he is not, there will be consequences."

"Yes."

"You will bear the brunt of them. Grange is your last operations officer. When he is retired, you will also be retired."

"I ... understand."

"Excellent. Keep me informed."

A bomb. What kind of vengeance wraith used a thrice-Christing bomb? Coughing on the smoke pouring from the window just feet away, Hiram grabbed the lip of the recessed ledge on which Saint Paul stood, giving quiet thanks for the extravagance of Catholics, and lowered himself until he hung at full stretch. His insides were ablaze, the fires centred around his ribs, and he could not bear to hang on long enough to judge the drop. Letting go of the slushy stone, fingertips already freezing, he fell, intending to take the impact through his knees, but his injured hip would not play. Buckling before he could roll, it pitched him onto his back in the snow and debris. Spluttering as he slid on the cobbles, he noted a pink mist spraying up from his lips with alarm.

Spectators were already gathering at either end of the alley, but he took his time getting to his feet. Being stared at in Polish was no different from being stared at in English, but at least he lacked the linguistic ability to have to explain the situation. Propping himself against the church wall, noting with a groan the amount of blood smeared into his snow angel outline on the ground, he nodded curtly at the priest who poked his head around the door further along. Glancing up at the shattered apartment window above, where dust and smoke still trailed into the night as though seeking him out, he shook his head in weary admiration. The explosives had been set with an expert knowledge and attention to detail. None of the other flats in the building were damaged, the charges having had a more incendiary than concussive kick. His rooms would be ablaze, but there was plenty of time for an evacuation. On cue, a fire alarm screeched out, the smoke reaching the detectors in the hallway. Those in his own apartment had been fried.

What kind of vengeance wraith gave careful thought to minimising the collateral damage of its attacks? Why had it rigged his only escape route as the trigger, ensuring that he would be halfway to freedom before the bomb went off? It could have set the charges to be detonated by remote, and waited for its pet driver to signal that Hiram was trapped. He would be charred bone and melting flesh by now. It was both an expert assassination attempt, and a grossly incompetent one.

Bending with a whimper, all of his injuries screaming with fresh vigour, he scooped up a handful of snow and rubbed it into his face. The chill felt good, and he walked slowly around the building, one trailing hand dragging on the wall in case he needed support. In the end, despite feeling like a marionette in the hands of a toddler, he did not. Rage colder than the Polish snow gave him artificial strength. As he turned the corner, he passed three young women running from the main road to see what had happened. One, a redhead with scarlet eyeliner, dressed in a black corset beneath her parka, stopped. "*Wszystko dobrze?*"

"Unless you're inviting me to join you in a recuperative foursome," he said, ignoring the soft bubbling in his throat that made him sound like a talkative frog, "I'm afraid I must decline." She stepped back, appalled, her English clearly better than he had assumed, but there was only one woman of real interest to him in that moment. As he pushed on toward the front of the building, he saw that same woman waiting for him at the entrance to the side street. The swirling snow masked the detail of her, but he recognised the square line of her shoulders beneath the ankle-length PVC coat. The taut power of her body was unmistakable, even so concealed. Above a face hidden by a high collar, dyed black hair blew around in the rising wind, the only movement in her impassive silhouette.

She watched him watching her, and his suspicions were confirmed. Gabrysia Kedra wanted him alive, and everything that had gone before was point scoring. She turned as he moved towards her, vanishing behind the snow, and he quickened his pace, his rage tempered now by fear of the discoveries he might soon make.

The crowd in front of the building was focused on the arched doorway leading into the inn, fully open now, and Hiram emerged onto the street unchallenged. All eyes were on the tourists stumbling from within, tendrils of smoke reaching gently after them. Guilt was a rare sensation for him, as injured bystanders were usually those who would be dead anyway without his intervention, but this was different. If there had been deaths here, he would have borne responsibility for them, as he was the only reason chaos had descended on these people.

They were all Sadie, to one degree or another.

It occurred to him that the fault may not lie with him alone, not this time, for Bothwell had put him there. She had much to answer for. Perhaps more than he had ever realistically believed possible.

Buttoning his coat with fumbling fingers, he scanned the street, placing Kedra outside the club he had noted earlier. As soon as she saw him watching, she stepped inside. It was to be a public meeting. Hiram felt for his gun, embarrassed that he had not checked it after his rapid exit from the apartment. Feeling its weight in his coat pocket, he approached the door, another archway, glass-fronted this time, and leading to another large interior courtyard with three doors. One was what appeared to be a combined tattoo and suntan parlour. It made sense, he supposed, to bring two arts of self-mutilation together in one handy outlet. A second door was a store selling prints and ancient movie posters, the usual *Taxi Driver*, Dali, and Escher exhibits on display.

The last door, on his left, was the entrance to the club, a door leading to a stairway down. As the driver steered him through the city, he had seen several such bars. Subterranean drinking was all the rage in Krakow. At the door, a muscular, shaven-headed bouncer was in animated discussion with a whip-thin blond girl. Hiram approached, wishing he had a mirror to check his appearance. The man's eyes widened a little at the sight of him, and he raised a finger at the girl. "Shush Lucy," he said, and then to Hiram. "You are coming in?"

Hiram nodded, aware of the Webley's bulk in his pocket. This was going to be an interesting pat down.

Instead of insisting that he spread-eagle, the bouncer pulled a slip of paper from his pocket and checked the handwritten scrawl there. "Your name?"

Hiram dithered a moment, then caught up. The apartment had never been booked by Bothwell. He had been hijacked from the start, and placed in Kedra's heartland. "Hiram Grange."

The bouncer nodded, his reluctance evident. "You are on guest list."

"How fortunate for me."

"You go in. Toilet is at foot of stairs. You wash. Blood frightens customers. You have much blood."

"Point taken." Hiram stepped past the couple, feeling their gazes burning into the back of his neck as he descended on rubber legs. As promised, there was a washroom at the bottom. The mirrors above the row of sinks proved the bouncer well-founded in his fears. Hiram looked like a macabre artwork, flesh as alabaster as his good friend Saint Paul, but speckled with vibrant reds. A quick wash made him only faintly less hideous, but he stepped into the club proper with renewed purpose. The bar had taken to its underground theme with gusto, the lighting a mix of neon blues and purples, and in different circumstances he might have considered it an ideal hunting ground for the sort of carnal pleasures he most enjoyed. The first room he entered was a bar, the lights above it a white beacon in the gloom. There was no sign of Kedra, so he took a seat on a stool shaped like a cupped, golden hand. The next room through was a dance floor, and music pounded through the doorway in solid pulses.

A barmaid saw him waiting, and brought a glass of single malt Scotch without him asking. She pointed to a table behind him, to one side of the door he had just come through. Kedra sat there, waiting for him. He had walked straight past her. The painkillers, he decided, were playing hell with his reflexes, once again giving the bitch an opportunity to spare his life. She was on familiar ground, and had the skills to turn that to her advantage.

Point taken. Again.

She nodded as he pulled out a chair opposite her, keeping the table between them. Her pale blue eyes were severe. "I am glad you live," she said, though her tone was so neutral he could not judge her sincerity.

He raised his glass. "Your very brief health. Why am I alive?"

"Because you are starting to believe. What did she tell you I was? Vampyre? Were? Faerie?"

"Rusalka," he said, and giving voice to that lie forced him to accept that in this, at least, Bothwell had misled him. The flicker in Kedra's eyes as he said it was interesting. A buzz passed over his loins at her moment of doubt and vulnerability. She looked so like his Jodie—a violin-wire frame of neat, unobtrusive muscle, thin, seductive lips, ethereal eyes. Her chin was stronger, her nose more full, but she was in many ways a perfect, lethal facsimile.

"How much do you believe?"

There was the rub, and he stroked thin fingers across his lips. "Are we secure here?"

"From who? Your masters?"

He nodded, uneasy even at the suggestion that he was complicit in hiding from Bothwell.

"As secure as we can be. Not very secure."

"There will be …"

"Cleanup teams at the apartment? *Nie.* You are wrong. The Office has only you left here."

Hiram drummed his fingers on the table, trying to ignore the implications of that statement. "Very well." He was decided. "I believe you."

"You do?"

"Wait. No." It was too much. "I believe that you believe. For some reason, you think Bothwell works for some secretive cabal, instead of running one. You think that you are … like me."

"Like you? I do not think so."

"Why, thank you."

"*Rzeczownik*. My former suffering is something you cannot understand. I was dragged from hell, pulled into new life when nothing made sense. They gave structure, training. They gave purpose. Only in this are we same."

Hiram bristled at her dismissal of his trials. His mother's suicide, his father's abandonment, his cursed quest into the shadows, desperate for answers. Piercing the veil, his heart melting at what was beyond it. The madness that followed, before Bothwell found him. The madness since. Elise. Sadie. Countless more. So many names, so many dead.

It all seemed so long ago.

"You dismiss me in ignorance, madam."

"We all suffer. Suffering pushes us against veil. They find us at our worst, whisper half-true *things*, make us their killing toys."

Hiram slugged his whisky, the burn a glorious distraction from his whirling thoughts. Her self-deceit was a glorious construct, an epic thing he was reluctant to interfere with. It sounded so plausible. "So if you are like me, where is your support? I have Bothwell, she has her cleanup crews, her spies, her admin support. Where is your Bothwell?"

She winced. "Pierre. He had analysts, surveillance people, more. All dead now. It has been *busy* two years."

Hiram went cold. "You killed them. Is that what you're telling me?"

"They lied to me. I do not like men who lie to me." How very gender specific, and no wonder Bothwell wanted her dead.

No. Closing his eyes, he chased the thought away. That was not the reason, could not be the reason. If Pierre and his team had been slaughtered by this woman, then they were real. If they were real, he would have to give equal weight to other parts of the story. He could not allow that. Hiram knew he was unique, that his traumas had been for a greater good. What else could he believe? That he had been abandoned so young through cruel, random chance? Yet, there was no harm in playing along, gathering what intel he could about her motivations and beliefs. "Did they have to die? Does it make so big a difference that there are others in the world fighting the same fight as you, winning the war a little faster? I have put down many evils, but another three step into each gap I create. I fight a losing battle. Why should we be so afraid of finding companions on the road?"

She rolled her eyes, catching him in the lie. Of course he understood her fear. He would share it, if anything she had told him were true. By playing 'what if,' he gained a sense of what life would be like for him in her version of reality. He would feel eroded, smaller than before, and in his confusion and insecurity might also choose to lash out.

Yes. He would tear the world apart in his rage. How glad he was that she was wrong on every count.

"You still have doubts? You have seen who I am, what I do, and you still think I could be *szaleniec*?"

With a grimace, he let a wave of exhaustion slump his shoulders. He did not know what she was, only what she could not be. "Miss Kedra, in the last day I have been dropped from the sky by a man-bat, flown most of the way across the world, kidnapped, and latterly, thanks to you, blown up. I'm tired. I'm hurt. I want to kill you." She tensed, fingers slipping beneath her coat. "I won't, don't worry. I don't know what parts of your story to believe, but if you wanted me dead, I would be in the ground by now."

"*Tak*. I mean, yes."

"May I ask you a question?"

"Anything."

"When I told you that Bothwell led me to believe you were a rusalka, you reacted. Why was that?"

She leaned forward, elbows on the table. "Local problem. Young men, dead on the banks of Vistula. Naked, drained of juices. You understand? I believe rusalka is responsible."

Hiram nodded, also leaning forward on his elbows. "I see," he spoke softly, matching her tone. Bothwell had chosen the rusalka with care. Given a chance to research the creature, he would have seen reports of the deaths, accepted them as evidence against Kedra. "That makes sense." He leaned a little closer, surprised at the sudden, easy sense of intimacy between them. "Can I ask another?" She nodded. "If you are like me, as you claim, then why is it still alive?"

She held his gaze a moment, then found the tabletop more interesting. "It does no harm," she said.

Hiram raised an eyebrow. "Explain."

"It kills abusers. Rapists. Paedophiles. *Monsters*." The venom in her voice spread across her face in creases, showing something ugly beneath the surface. Hiram shook his head, the intimacy dissipating as he sat back.

"It kills people. That is enough. Your claims are false. You are *nothing* like me." He stood, knowing all he needed to reassure himself. "Good day, madam."

"Where are you going?"

"I was sent here to kill a rusalka. My mission has not changed."

She grabbed his arm. "Missions, objectives, but you see nothing of their meaning."

"I'm tired of riddles."

"Why kill it? Because your Bothwell wishes it so? Rusalka preys on predators. It is no different from you, from me. It is not evil, it is justice." Standing, barely as tall as his collarbone, she stepped close, so that he could feel the feverish heat of her. "Hold, for tonight. Rest. There is more to say. You know only first lie." Despite his injuries, the leaden tiredness in him, he responded to her closeness. Looking at her upturned face, now strangely vulnerable, he wondered how aware she was of his arousal, and whether she was using it against him.

Rest would be good. A bed to sleep in, a woman to drain into. "One night," he said. "Then there will be killing."

"Agreed." As she led him from the bar, he had the impression they were no longer discussing entirely the same thing.

Kedra led him back onto the street, where the driving snow sucked heat from him like an arctic vampire, then to his surprise took him back to the same building he had so recently escaped. There was a fire crew outside, and she spoke rapid, vowel-free Polish to an officer by the door. He nodded, waving them inside. Hiram followed, careful not to tread on the hose draping up the stairs. At the first floor, two more officers nodded them past his former apartment. Smoke still laced the air, but he assumed the fire was out and the building declared structurally sound.

There was only one door on the second floor, and Kedra unlocked it, leading him in. Now he understood why she had taken such care with the selection and placement of the explosives—she had been sitting above him the entire time, waiting for the bomb to go off. As she locked the door behind them, he glanced around the huge apartment, the only one on this level. The sitting room was the same size as his whole flat had been, numerous doors leading off to what he assumed to be kitchen, bathrooms, bedrooms, and more. In the centre of the room was a vast couch, soft black leather over a solid timber frame, and she gestured him towards it. The bare floorboards were covered with strange sigils, wards and defences far more advanced than those sealing his Airstream in America. It first made him uncomfortable to acknowledge that she might be his better in some areas, and then irritated him that he insisted on dealing with her as though her story were true.

"I have Scotch, good vodka, gin. No absinthe. You wish to drink?"

"I do." He sat, the warm leather moulding around him. "Scotch and water, no ice." She hung her coat on a stand behind the door, endearingly sculpted to resemble human bones, then strode to a heavy, ornate drinks cabinet, looking suddenly casual in her faded grey jeans and vest top. He admired the pale skin of her neck and shoulders as it played over a fine network of muscles. There were scars on show—a long, ragged one curving from her right shoulder to her breast, and several on her left shoulder blade—circular blemishes that hinted at the liberal application of lit cigarettes. Whatever she had been through to become what she was, he did not doubt her claims of suffering.

Bringing his drink across, she took a seat alongside him, a generous vodka in her other hand. "Well," he said, "this is cosy."

She shrugged, and her scrutiny was like a physical rubdown. "You have not asked most obvious question."

"Really? I must be tired. What would that be?"

"Why I wish so much for you to believe me."

"I'll be honest." He leaned back into the couch. "I'm still struggling with the first principles of your story."

"Yes. You should know, anyway."

"Very well. There are a series of … what? Operatives? Agents? Officers?"

"Agents is good. Three. Me. You. One other."

Hiram sipped his whisky, nodding. "Three then. We have been lied to about the agency we work for, denied knowledge of each other's existence. Yet our purpose has not changed. We protect humanity."

Kedra snorted. "*Nie*. We endanger it."

"By wiping evil from the world?"

"By eliminating competition."

Something nasty clicked into place in Hiram's head. Exhausted beyond reason, wishing he had never set foot in Poland, he took a deep breath. "What?"

"We eliminate competition. We clear way for the one who walks in white, the worst of all. We deliver world to evil."

Hiram's mouth was dry, the room suddenly too large, his agoraphobia surging to the fore. "Don't be ridiculous."

"Anything that threatens him, that could spoil his *ambicja* …

his ambition, is eliminated. We kill for him, like mad dogs loosed."

"I would know."

"You believe is so? Ten years, I killed things Pierre told me to kill. I wanted purpose, I did not question. When did you last ask your Bothwell *why*? Not what, or how, or where, but *why*?"

"I … people die. I stop the things that kill them."

"Pah." She was close enough that her plosive brushed over his lips as warm, vodka-scented air. "People die. What of it? Sometimes men are predators. Sometimes prey." Hiram followed her logic, too well. A flutter of panic danced in his lungs, and he wished he had his pipe to quell it. "I was used. You are used. We are toys. I cannot take him alone. With you, perhaps there is small chance."

Hiram shook his head, appalled at where her delusions would take him. This conversation had to end, immediately. Placing his hand behind her head, he pulled her forcibly to him, meeting the surprised 'O' of her lips with his own. She tasted of cloves and smelled of lilac. It was wonderful.

Her fist found his cracked rib, jabbing it with one hard knuckle extended. Falling back with a cry, needles of pain slicing through him, he was aware of her standing over him, knife in hand.

The fire in her eyes died to a simmer, and she threw the weapon at a chipped board hanging on the wall. It stuck there, tip first, and he doubted it was an accident that, if he were standing, it would be fixed at a height approximate to his crotch. "Sleep," she ordered, fists still clenched. "We talk in morning. You are tired. Your judgement is poor. I let you live." Turning, she strode through a door on the left, presumably a bedroom, and left him to his recovery.

She was taking hard-to-get to impressive lengths. Head spinning at all she had told him, he stretched gingerly out on the couch, fishing his wallet from his pocket. He needed to calm his nerves, so from behind a mystifying assortment of Euros, he pulled out his battered Polaroid of Jodie. Banishing all other thoughts, he loosened his trousers and masturbated to gentle release.

Afterwards, settled, he found that sleep was glad to have him.

"*Where?*"

"*We do not know. She has a base somewhere, that she sourced herself.*"

"*What of the Seer?*"

"*She cannot find them through the storm. She cannot move between the falling snow.*"

"*But he is with her?*"

"*Our best guess, nothing more.*"

"*Then he is lost.*"

"*You assume too much.*"

"*And you too little.*"

"*He may kill her yet. Whatever she has told him, it can all be undone if he takes her life.*"

"*At great effort, vast expense.*"

"*Greater than finding another like him? Starting again?*"

"I will not be swayed."

"You will open the confluence?"

"It is ever open. I will stoke it like a dying blaze, shake it like a wasp nest, and see what flies free. We shall remind him of his purpose. If he survives, then I will consider his position."

"Very well. I stand ready."

Hiram woke in darkness, fully alert, and knew something was wrong. Opening his eyes a sliver, he moderated his breathing, ignoring the burn of his wounds, the locked stiffness of his muscles.

Somebody was watching him, a slim, motionless shadow by the door. Kedra?

No, the outline lacked her poised sharpness, yet it remained familiar. There was a scent on the air, sweet and musky. It floated to him, filling him up, and he realised he had a powerful erection. Forcing his body into smooth response despite its myriad complaints, he sat up, pulling the Webley from his coat. The thing in the corner, girl-shaped now that his eyes had started to adjust, could only be one thing. Rusalka.

"Come closer," he told it, wanting to see this thing that made his face flush and his heart beat faster by its mere presence. He always looked into the dark things, seeking the peace and beauty he had glimpsed long ago, terrified of what might happen if he found it.

The shape stepped forward. It wore a young woman's body, and nothing else. A thrill went through him as he saw the slim, pale belly, the firm young breasts. This, then, was how the lure worked, and he ignored the promise of pleasure that made his bruised flesh tingle. If he kept his focus, he would not succumb. The creature's head was down, her jet black hair covering her face. The sense of familiarity was almost as strong as his sexual need. Part of the trap, he guessed, a secondary lure should the promise of swift orgasm be insufficient.

It reached the middle of the room, and he stared at the slight slump of the shoulders, the sweet, coy tilt of its head. His mouth dried as he recognised his error. The creature was familiar, not due to some mystical lure for the foolhardy, but because he actually *knew* it. Afraid now, he thumbed back the hammer of the Webley, knowing he should have killed it already, desperate to blow its face away before he had to see it.

Too late. It raised its head, and became a she.

Sadie.

Hiram's gun arm wavered as her eyes implored him. Sadie, his friend. Her lips parted, and she mouthed his name. Sadie, the girl he had never touched, for fear of souring something wholly good. Her nipples hardened before his eyes, her breasts as perfect as he had once imagined. Sadie, the girl who became too important, too precious to cast aside with cruel sex, regardless how often he fantasised it. Sadie. The girl he had killed.

"You're dead," he said, as she lowered herself to her knees before him. She tilted her head to look at him, hair falling away from a once playful face. Nodding, the lust in her eyes something he had never seen before, she waited.

There was a clatter, what might have been his gun falling from his hand, but he was too lost to be sure. "I failed you," he said, shame joining the flood of arousal in his veins. His erection was agony, threatening to crush itself to pulp against his trousers, so he freed it with fumbling fingers. She bobbed forward, a dog being teased with a treat, and kissed it with cool, velvet lips.

Was this what it would have been like?

She slid him into her mouth, pushing him into her throat and letting him rest there. His hands found her bare shoulders, sweet soft skin that he had never touched, and he whimpered as she swallowed around him. Something was wrong. At the very tip of him, there was a sensation like pain, as though she were penetrating him in turn, pushing into his shaft and tickling down the length. Her moist tongue swirled, and he ceased to care. Closing his eyes, he saw her death, his own Webley at her temple, his finger on the trigger. As her tongue worked, and that other part of her pushed deeper into him, he lost himself to sensation. For her to be here, to do this, felt like forgiveness.

Or revenge.

Opening his eyes, fighting euphoria, he saw things as they were, visualised himself standing in Kedra's room as something buried itself in him. "No." He barely raised his voice, but Sadie stiffened, and the thing inside wriggled as though searching for purchase. It hurt, but in such a sweet, divine way that the strength vanished from his legs. He collapsed back onto the couch, and she followed, clamped to him like a leech.

It could not be Sadie. She had died in the basement of the *UberNacht*, thousands of miles away, having never had the chance to leave America, see the world for herself. For her to turn up here, a vengeful wraith slaughtering men on the banks of the Vistula, made no sense.

He had no idea where his gun was.

Gasping, fear riding on the back of pleasure and steering it to new heights, he placed his hands on either side of her head as the burrowing tube inside him reached the base of his cock. He felt it twitch, as though looking for something, then it latched down, and impossible sensations washed through him. Whimpering, eyes rolled back in his head, he tried to move his arms, pull her away, but he was no longer in charge. By latching to him, she had seized possession of his limbs, and to his horror he watched his hands gently caressing her hair as his hips bucked gently against her mouth. His balls tingled, clenched. If he came, he was certain he would die.

Kedra was there before he heard her, pale and naked. Bearing witness to her lithe, scarred nudity almost pushed him beyond the point of no return. Only the sneer of contempt on her lips saved him. Grabbing the rusalka by the hair, she yanked it away. Hiram screamed as something tore inside, that long, needling tube scraping free with sickening speed. As he took control of his limbs again, blood splattering from his penis to the floor, he watched as Kedra dragged the thing away, a long, black straw whipping back into its mouth. Sadie looked at him, eyes pleading, and despite himself he raised a weak hand to Kedra.

If she saw him, she ignored his plea, shoving the barrel of a Colt automatic to Sadie's temple. "Wait," he said, but she didn't, pulling the trigger with a small grunt that was swallowed by the gunshot. The black ooze that blasted out of Sadie's opposite temple did not come from a human being, but still Hiram's heart broke as she slumped to the floor.

Dead, because of him, all over again.

Kedra spat on the corpse. "A little silver through bullet. Not worth it, I think." Hiram's strength was returning slowly, and that was a good thing, because if he were already fully recovered he could have coldly killed her. From the look on Kedra's face, the feeling was reciprocated. "Put cock away. Is embarrassing." He did so, not looking down to see the damage done. For some reason, he felt very strongly that he should not take his eyes off hers. After blazing with the kill, they had dulled, and now regarded him with unblinking contemplation.

"I will not apologise. It had power. Some sort of control over men."

"*Tak*," she said, blunt and quiet. "Pheromones. Big dose, seeping through skin."

"More than that. She saw into my mind, pulled out the face of a girl I once knew, and wore it."

"*Nie.*"

"Yes. She looked like Sadie. A friend."

"You are wrong. Rusalka cannot shift skin. They are spirits of girls who died in violence. They return to kill killers."

Hiram wanted to cry. "No," he said, but it was true. Sadie had sought him out because he had killed her.

Kedra raised her gun, locking a steady aim between his eyes, and he froze. "I was there. I pulled you from burning club, and saw her body. I did not see her die. What did you do to her?"

"What?"

"How did she die?"

"I thought you were seeking an ally. This is not leading to a healthy working relationship."

"I do not work with monsters. You hurt her. Was rape? Torture?"

"No!" He took a steadying breath. "She was my friend. I tried to save her."

"For this, she wanted you dead? I do not think so. Tell me, or I finish you for her."

"If she had never met me, never decided there was something of worth in me and tried to touch it, she would not have been exposed to my world." It was the first time he had tried to put words to her death, because nobody had asked before. "She was dragged into my wake, and died because I was weak. Yes, I killed her. I wish you hadn't pulled me out of the fire. I wish I'd burned with her corpse." His cheeks were wet, but he refused to acknowledge his tears by wiping them away.

Kedra studied his grief, and lowered her gun. "*Tak*, I understand how such things come to be." The weight of personal pain behind her simple statement made it clear she was remembering more than empathising. "I will dress." She pointed at a chest beneath one window. "Blankets, for body."

Hiram nodded as she returned to her room, grateful for the moment's privacy. As soon as she closed the door, he released a ragged breath, crouching beside the tiny body. Death always made things smaller. "I always wondered whether you would blame me," he said, leaning forward to kiss her cheek, stroke her belly. "Now I know."

When Kedra returned, wearing black jeans and a form-hugging black polo neck, Hiram was checking over his Webley. Satisfied, he slipped it into his pocket as she scanned the room. "She's in the chest," he said. "I didn't want to clutter the place up."

She stared. Nodded. "Is good. Later, we move her. Now we have trouble."

"Do we?"

She nodded, walking to the door, giving curt examination to the wards around it.

"She came in here?"

"Yes."

"Impossible."

"My bleeding penis says not."

"The sigils are intact. Rusalka is weak thing. It could not have got in."

Hiram shook his head, feeling slow and stupid. What was wrong with him? "Yet she did. Another thing. I don't think that Sadie is your rusalka. She might have crossed the world to see me dead, but why would she have been here before me? How long have men been turning up dead by the river?"

She nodded. "*Tak.* Too long. Is no sense."

Despite the earlier mauling, Hiram's penis struggled back to painful life in her presence. He shifted his stance as he watched her stalk the room. To distract himself, he checked the sigils for himself, aware of her sudden scrutiny. Brushing his fingers over one arcane symbol, he felt the dull throb of power within. She was right. The rusalka should not have breached this, yet it had. "Where would it get the power from to pass by this?"

"There is one place only. You are aroused."

The stark non sequitur made him blink. "My apologies."

"Is me?"

"While I appreciate the interest, your timing is questionable."

"Have I made cock hard?" There was nothing playful about the question, and after a dullard moment, he realised why. Stepping back from the door, he cursed his idiocy. "No. Not you." She nodded, drawing the Colt. "Lingering pheromones from my friend in the box?" His own flippancy carried him over the pain and guilt.

"*Nie*, is dead. No more pheromones."

Hiram's heart was pumping too fast, and his mouth dried. "Another, then. It's stronger than the last one," he said, joining her in the centre of the room. "More potent."

"I think not." He stared at her lips, and the invite in their flex and moisture. She slapped him with her free hand, rocking him on his heels, but he was glad of it. "Clear your mind," she said.

He nodded, pride preventing him from rubbing his jaw, and checked the window, keeping low. Through the snow he saw women in the streets, motionless, staring up at him. Their pull was strong, and his vision swirled. His mind fogged, and he wanted to show himself, offer his body to their hands and mouths.

"They are many?"

"Very many." He struggled to remember how to count. "Ten. No. Twelve. More. Kedra, I …"

She pulled him back into the room, turning him to face her. "You will look at me at all times." The flicker in her eyes could almost have been concern. "You go where I go, do as I say."

"While I love the femdom thing you have going on there,

I … they're strong."

"*Tak*. They make promises to your body that it wants to accept." Hiram nodded. "I make promise, too. When this night ends, if you live, you will have me. You understand this?" Her urgency arrested his wandering thoughts. Something beneath her words hinted that this was neither a casual promise, nor an easy one. "Take shallow breaths. Focus desire on me."

"Easy."

"Maybe yes, maybe no. Perhaps too many pheromones make your heart stop, and I will not have to keep my promise."

"You flirt."

She smiled, for the briefest moment girlish. "Is good. Follow me." Taking his hand, she led him to the bedroom. Before he could think of a joke, he saw the ladder on the back wall, and the hatch in the ceiling. "Up," she said. "Is not long before they see they can get in." At the top, he punched the wooden hatch open and hoisted himself onto the flat roof. The first breath of fresh air helped him reorder his muddled thoughts. While his flesh still hungered for debauchery, the effect was lessened. Whether this was because he was further above the rusalka, or because the pheromones had been more concentrated trapped between four walls, he neither knew nor cared. Snow gusted around him, and the icy wind dimmed the fire in his blood still further. Kedra joined him, bolting the hatch at her feet.

"What good will that do?" He had to fight the wind to make himself heard. "However Sadie got in, she didn't use the door."

"I do not know. Rusalka should be bound to flesh, not walk through walls. Something has stirred confluence, gives them power."

"I didn't know they could be used like that." The thought

appalled him. The confluences were gates, waxing and waning, usually spilling preternatural discharge at random. That they could be used in so specific and targeted a way, that somebody could be so crazed and powerful as to even try, terrified him. "Who?"

"Your master, who walks in white and craves dominion. He knows I have told you. He cannot let us live." Hiram shook his head, but the denial was now only a reflex. She touched his arm. "Later, we talk. Plan. We stop him, before he takes everything, yes?" Numb from more than the cold, he nodded. "Wait here." Crouching, she ran to the roof edge, sure footed over the ice.

Hiram watched, taking shallow breaths as he had been told. The black clouds above had found their way into his heart, and a storm was brewing inside. Bothwell had been his saviour, picking him up from the ruins he had made of his life, pointing his grief and rage at humanity's enemies, and letting him tear them down. Except, it had not been that way at all. By exploiting his grief, she had dishonoured him, used his mother's death against him, made his tragedies sad, diminished shackles that bound him mindlessly to her purpose.

No longer. He was going to survive the night, and there would be a reckoning.

Gritting his teeth, embracing the heat of his anger and forging it into new purpose, he joined Kedra. She was motionless, and a quick glance down told him why. The street was full of women, two dozen at least. Kedra sensed him beside her, put out her hand to wave him back, but it was too late.

As soon as he glanced down, they looked up in unison, a bizarre, synchronous gesture that scared him to the core. Then the lust shot into him. He had time to wonder whether hormones could be aimed, and then need took his breath away, stole his thoughts, sucked the strength from his limbs. Kedra grabbed him, pulling him back when he wanted to drop forwards.

What came after was made of snapshots, broken strips of film spliced together in a jumbled montage.

Kedra shoves and pulls him across the roof, screams words he doesn't understand, and he doesn't remember why he is there, why they can't simply stop, and strip, and suck.

Another rooftop, tiled and slanted, and there are other women behind him, but the one he wants pulls him away, slipping and sliding, ice water soaking into their clothes.

A ladder to the street, and at the bottom he is submerged in primeval lust. Grabbing the woman he is with, shoving her against a wall, he has one hand on her throat as he mauls her breasts with the other, the fear in her eyes spurring him on, and now she has squirmed free, is taunting his need, leading him along the street, and frustration makes him roar.

Another street, onto a vast square where snow has room to twirl and dance, and she eludes him still, slipping from his reaching fingers, gun in hand as she glances past him over and again. Turning, seeing for himself the desperate, pleading women following, slinking along walls, trotting after, bowed low by a need to match his own, some dressed, others gloriously naked, snowflakes melting on flesh, and if the one he wants is so desperate to elude him, then these others can feast.

Stepping towards the nearest, a huge-breasted redhead whose face melts with pleasure that she is chosen, he hears desperate wails from the others as he tears open his coat, fumbles with his shirt. A small hand grips his collar from behind as the redhead drops to all fours and scuttles forward, her tongue flicking. A gun appears over

his shoulder. He is pulled back as the gun goes off, and is glad to be dead and have the madness end, except the bullet is not for him, and the redhead grows a third fountaining eye as the shot deafens him. Disorientation replaces lust, and he remembers enough to follow Kedra at a run towards a dual-towered red brick church at the square's edge. More women pour into the square from other streets, impossible numbers, and he loses himself again.

Inside the church, his woman screams at men in black with white at their throats, waving her gun as they flee, barring the door behind them. Stained glass, and gold, and sad, painted saints and martyrs surround him as he drags her to the central aisle, determined now to take her. Pain as she punches him hard, forcing him to release her, but then her small, sure hands are in his trousers, freeing him, and she turns him away from her as she presses into his back, one hand reaching round and pumping him, the other training the gun on the door as she works him faster, and his testicles clench, and pleasure spits from him.

Hiram screamed, remembering his name, his purpose, as his semen splashed to the cold stone floor. Kedra's partial embrace held him up as she continued to work him, emptying him as fully as she could. "Enough!" She let go, and he staggered on legs like jelly.

"It worked, yes?" She sounded desperate, and when he could bring himself to look back at her, he saw exhaustion written on her face.

"How long were we out there?"

"Too long. They are too many. I could not keep control."

"Of them, or me?" He pulled a tissue from his pocket, wiping himself before offering it to her.

"You remember nothing?" She cleaned her hand with an absent-minded precision that looked long practised.

"Nothing." It seemed the politic thing to say.

"Lust is gone?"

"No, but it's dim. Waiting to build. Where are we?"

"St Mary's Basilica. Very old. Big tourist attraction."

"Delightful." In the gloom, with the strange, multi-toned light from the elaborate windows, the church was enchanting in a way that clashed with what she had just done to, and for, him. "A lovely setting for our first dalliance."

"You think more is coming?"

"You promised. The morning, remember?"

She raised her eyebrows, passing him the tissue and pointing at the mess he had made on the flagstones. "*Tak*. I did."

Hiram stooped, wiping up his seed. "God will not approve. There might be smiting."

"God is not here tonight."

"You think so? Something's keeping the rusalka out."

"Memory and fear. They remember stories of churches as sanctuary."

"The power of reputation."

"It will not hold them. They will breach walls."

Done with mopping the floor, he looked for a bin, saw none, and placed the tissue gingerly back into his pocket. "Then we need to go, before my lusts take me again. Because they will, believe me." Slumping in a pew, he fastened his shirt, not entirely clear about when he had unbuttoned it in the first place. "I have a window, I think. I can help get us out."

"Good. I have idea where we must go."

"Do tell."

"These creatures are directed. We have passed many people, but rusalka do not turn aside. For them, is you and only you."

"And I thought it was my animal magnetism. Is it this man in white?"

"Behind things, yes. Providing power, manipulating confluences, yes. Nobody else. Controlling things here, no. Is too close. Something local, I think. Like rusalka, but stronger."

"How do we find it?"

"A guess only, but they are water creatures. We look to the Vistula."

For want of a better idea, he nodded. "No time like the present, my dear. Do you need to catch your breath?"

"*Nie*. Do you?"

"Oh yes. I'm exhausted, broken, and in tremendous pain. Could we ask them to give us an hour or two before they storm the church?"

She smiled, and he felt a worrying flicker of arousal. "We could ask."

"Alas, I'm having urges. I can't tell if it's you or them."

"I take no offence."

He rose, pulling his Webley free as she reloaded her Colt. Ready, they exchanged a weary glance and trudged to the barred side door. Beyond the dark, aged wood the gale howled, and below that, a low disappointed moan of frustration issued from dozens of soft throats. Hiram steeled himself. "Time to sally forth." He had no idea how his body was going to react, but before he could consider further, she slid the bolts back and flipped the door open.

The rusalka had been pressed against it, a pack of them blocking the way out. From where he stood, he could not tell how far back they went, and as he raised his gun he wondered if he had enough bullets. Warmth grew in his loins, but after Kedra's ministrations he was unable to grow hard. For the first time in his life, he was grateful to be so unresponsive. "Mow them down," he shouted, the wind whistling past him and stealing the thunder from his order. Kedra followed his lead, taking aim at each face in turn and putting a careful bullet in it, the thunder of gunfire drowning even the gale. The rusalka dropped before them, and as each fell they kicked the body back beyond the door, leaving the exit free. The Webley was done before the Colt, clicking empty on the sixth chamber, and the filed-down cartridge left there in remembrance of his mother. Having allowed lies to dishonour her, his resolve to make amends was a steel support deep within. Grabbing the door, he waited for Kedra's last shot, then pulled her back and slammed it shut.

The acoustics in the church had captured the blare of their weapons, and boomed the fading soundtrack back at them as they reloaded. "How many more?" Kedra said.

"Plenty, and more arriving. We're not going to be able to put them all down. We need to push through."

"*Tak*. We separate, go across square. We meet on far side. Do not wait for me."

He nodded, raised the Webley, and threw back the door. New faces leered at him, and he pressed the barrel against the forehead of a too-young blonde. The shot threw her back, the bullet passing through her skull and punching through the cheek of the one behind, spinning it back and left. Stepping into the gap their violent departure created, he felt hands on him, and realised the game had changed. They were no longer seducing him. Now they were attacking. They had sensed the failure of their allure, and were taking a more direct approach. Their controller was close, keeping abreast of developments, determined to have him one way or another. Had his release in the church been witnessed? The thought made him feel dirty, but he consoled himself with the now straightforward battle. Throwing an elbow into the throat of a rusalka on his left, he slammed the butt of the Webley into the face of a chubby brunette in front of him, shattering its nose. Both fell away reeling, and he knew he had a chance. The rusalka were lovers, not fighters.

Conserving ammunition, he ducked and weaved, arms and legs lashing out, bringing the creatures down as he pushed forward, more concerned now with breaking free of the pack than putting them down permanently. What they lacked in skill and strength, they made up for with numbers, and time blurred as his injuries lit up and the chill of the snow and wind sapped his energy. Unable to seduce, the creatures still aimed for the areas they knew best, scratching at his lips, jabbing at his crotch and nipples, as though resentful of his rejection. One nimble teen threw herself catlike onto his back, sinking her teeth into his neck. Roaring, he reached over his shoulder, grabbing her as he twisted, flipping her forward. Blood dribbled down his throat as she took a chunk of flesh away, and he hurled her at the next two, staggering as the three of them crashed to the ground, sliding over the snowy cobbles.

There was nobody behind them. Seizing the opportunity, he raced into the square. A glance over his shoulder made his jaw drop—there were dozens of them milling in confusion in the shadow of the towering church. A couple had seen him, were running in drunken pursuit, but the rest were confused, still seeking him in their midst.

There was no sign of Kedra, but he took her at her word. If she was fighting free, he would see her on the far side. If she had fallen, he would avenge her. With his life in flames, it was all the same to him. Tomorrow, if he was alive to see it, would bring the chance to rebuild, to redefine himself, and in the grand scheme of things the loss of Kedra would be a tiny thing, regrettable, but inconsequential.

Putting his remaining strength into a sprint, he aimed for the end of the long building in the middle of the square. Krakow's celebrated Cloth Hall, he suspected, the arches along the side shuttered up for the night. Sealing themselves in the church had drawn the rusalka to that single point, and from what little he could see there were no more in the square. The two behind him were a problem, for he couldn't build up the speed to outdistance them. Putting them down might draw the attention of the rest of the pack, but there was nothing else to be done.

Reaching the great, square end of the Cloth Hall, he paused beneath the ornate clock hanging over the entrance, leaning on the door to catch a chilled breath. Ignoring the exhausted tremble in his limbs, he turned and drew aim. The two rusalka were shapes in the storm, and he paused longer than he liked to be certain he had not fixed on late-night revellers. They were within fifteen feet of him before he knew for sure, and he snuffed them out with two quick, deafening shots. Their heads snapped back as they fell, and he wondered how the front pages of the local newspaper would read tomorrow. It was not his most subtle evening's work.

Not knowing whether the rest of the pack were coming, unable to see the church at all through the snowfall, he made himself pause, reloading as he savoured the precious moments of stillness. His left side was almost numb with pain, running from shoulder to hip. A slim female shape appeared behind him, and he cried out as he wrenched himself round to level the Webley. His finger slipped from the trigger as he tried to take the shot, but a second later he was glad of the error. "Kedra! Jesus woman, do you have a death wish?"

"*Żalujący*. I called out."

Perhaps she had. Exhaustion made him single-minded to the point of blotting out everything not immediately relevant, and he ached for a sweet sip of something obliterating. "I'm glad you made it." To his surprise, he realised he wasn't paying lip service to the sentiment. "What kept you?"

"I have been here, waiting. They did not want me." She could have gone, he realised. She could have let the rusalka have him while she either abandoned the destruction he had brought to her door, or sought out its architect and took him down.

"You really do want my help, don't you?"

"*Tak*. Is lonely, being only one who knows. Is frightening." It was a statement of absolute honesty, and he had a rare moment of human empathy, understanding what it would be like to have been in her position. Would he have been able to fight on, try to take the war to the man in white as she had? He did not think so. More likely, he would have disappeared, lost himself in drugs and absinthe and despair.

"You're not alone anymore." She nodded, uncertain how to respond. "Now, don't we have an execution to be getting on with?"

She was clearly glad to move away from the brief moment of intimacy. "*Tak*. The war starts here."

"Yes. And it doesn't stop until the man in white is in the

ground. Let's move." Uncertain of the city's layout, he let her lead at a fast trot, past a huge iron head lying on its side, its hollow-eyed stare like that of some defeated winter god. Something for the tourists, made strange and sinister in the night. Clearing the square, she took him into narrow, ancient streets, past shivering drunks and occasional late-night clubs still throbbing with music. He grew slower as they ran, the limits of his body taking speed and sense from him. Outside a baroque Jesuit church fronted by twelve maudlin statues of the disciples, their aspects accusing him of failure, he staggered to a halt, wheezing and spitting blood into the new carpet of snow. Kedra sensed he had stopped, and returned to him. "You cannot do this," she said. "You have no fight left." There was no contempt in her statement, but his pride flinched anyway.

"I … I just need a moment. It's been … a long week."

"*Nie*. You die if you follow." The disciples above agreed from their lofty heights, aloof stares pitying.

A tingle buzzed across his nipples, and inside his pants he twitched. "I'll die if I stay." She tilted her head in query. "They're coming. I can feel them again. Not close, not yet, but heading this way."

"Not after us, I think. They do not know where we are. They return to their master. We chose right path."

"Well done us."

"Down this street is Wawel Hill, and the castle."

"The confluence?"

"Beneath the hill, beside the river."

"Into the dragon's den. I can't go back. I'm coming with you." She weighed it up, her reluctance evident. "*Tak*, is no choice."

"Then lead. Time passes." She did, starting at a walk to see if he could keep up. When he managed, force of will stopping him from staggering, she picked up the pace. The street sloped down, past coffee shops, and at the bottom they paused, squinting across the knot of roads that collided there. A looming shape lurked before them, and he knew they had reached Wawel Hill. Somewhere up there was a castle, hidden from view by the weather. That meant they were almost on top of the confluence, and he did not know whether the new prickle across his chest was from proximity to the thing, or a reaction to the closing pack of rusalka. He looked at Kedra for guidance. "Up?" He hoped not. He didn't know how much up his legs had in them.

"Around." She led on, crossing the traffic junction, ignoring the wide road carving up the side of the hill. Through the snow he saw flashes of battlements above, towers and spires beyond those. Finding a street edging round the base of the hill, which became a steep cliff once they passed the road leading up, they drew their coats tight, pressing on, knowing they were near the end.

Walking now, they found a tidy boulevard, and the water's edge. The Vistula. At the base of the hill, looking over the river, a metal statue of a dragon reared up, no doubt skinny and comical during the day, but stoically fearsome with snow piling on it, distorting the outline into something mutant and wrong.

Ice drifted in the swollen river. Snow rioted through the air. Hiram's teeth chattered. All else was still. "What now?"

Kedra pursed her lips. She seemed immune to the cold, but this was her home territory, the chill her friend. "Do they still follow?"

"I don't know. I can feel them, but they're not getting stronger. They could have been on us by now. I think they're keeping their distance."

"*Tak.* Is because …"

There was a splash from the river, and they turned to find the source, guns out before they had even registered the need. Ice on the currents, deadwood tumbling with it. There was no further sign of life, yet Kedra stiffened. "There," she said. Hiram squinted, trying to see something to concern him. There was nothing. Just the driftwood, and one larger log, drifting gently …

Hiram blinked. The log was floating towards them. Against the current. There was another splash, and this time he saw a glimpse of the arm that made it, algae green, black fish scales scattered across it. Whatever they had come for, it was swimming along behind that log. Kedra stared, unmoving, as it came for them. She seemed lost, and he grabbed her wrist, pulling her away from the river's edge, into the lee of the metal dragon. "Kedra?" She didn't hear him, and he shook her arm. "Gabrysia?" She looked at him, shock slackening her face, and he scowled. "This gives me no pleasure," he said, not entirely sure he was telling the truth. "Snap out of it," he said, slapping her across the cheek. He caught her as she stumbled over. "I need you here."

"*Dupek*," she said, and the venom in her voice was a welcome sign of recovery.

Another splash, and the log was nearly at the bank. "What is it?"

She couldn't take her eyes off the river, and he wanted to slap her again. She was not a woman who suited fear, and it made him feel horribly lost to see her wearing it. "Is wodnik. Water spirit. *Nie.* Water *god.* Is the Grandfather, the Vistula made flesh. Is doom."

"I've taken gods before. They're overrated."

She only shook her head, and he turned to see the log drifting away. A form rose up on the water, the river's muck sloughing from it as it ascended, until it stood on the river's surface as though it were solid ground. The creature had an old man's body, skin mottled, filthy hair and beard dripping. Its eyes were black with malice, and though it stood barely taller than Kedra, it reeked of power. Raising a wiry arm, it pointed a long, crusty fingernail at him.

"*You are the man Grange.*" Its voice was a gargle, the speech of the drowned. "*You must die. Why must you die, man Grange? Tell Grandfather why he must kill you?*"

Hiram took a step forward, and Kedra grabbed him, stopping him from going further. "Your enemy wishes it. The one in white. The one who would slaughter you and yours to own this." He pointed at the hill, and the confluence it concealed.

The Grandfather laughed, a mean, bubbling sound that crawled up Hiram's spine, tensing his shoulders. "*Enemy no more. He gives me confluence for you. He gives me pow-wer.*" It had yet to leave the river. A water god. Hiram's mind raced.

"He lies, little local god. He deceives. When we fall, he will come back here for you. Not tomorrow, perhaps. But I promise you, he will make this place his own."

The wodnik stilled, eyes empty as it harnessed its power. Behind it, the river moved, slowly at first, swirling in strange patterns. "*Come to me, man Grange. Join me at the riverbed. Serve me.*"

"Very tempting. Why don't you come over here? We can discuss terms and conditions."

It snarled, and the waters thrashed, ice crashing, impossible waves shooting up. "*The girl can be spared, be safe, so cosy. Come to me.*" The waves merged, spiralling upwards, a vast column of water. The wodnik raised its arms and paused, waiting for a response.

Hiram spat, a glob of blood and phlegm arcing through the snow and splashing against the creature's chest. "You overrate my sense of chivalry," he said.

The creature looked at the fluids on its chest, then shrieked, beard billowing, and brought its arms down. The column of water followed, breaking on the cliff above them before it crashed down, smashing them to the ground. A block of ice punched into his right arm, shattering it above the elbow. The deluge felt eternal, and he couldn't breathe as the ice water battered him, soaked him through, stole the last of his heat. He had no idea where Kedra was.

The downpour ceased. Gasping for air, bruised muscles leaden, he forced himself to sit up, clutching his ruined arm. The numbing cold from the drenching inured him to the pain a little, but he would be shooting left-handed for the foreseeable future.

Shots rang out. Still dazed, he first looked at his own hand to see if it was him. Already the chill was sapping him, as blood retreated to his vital organs, trying to keep them warm, trying to keep him alive. Struggling drunkenly to his feet, he watched Kedra emptying her Colt into the Grandfather. She still stood by the dragon statue, now fifteen feet away, and he realised he had been swept along the path. She must have grabbed the dragon and held on for dear life.

The Grandfather twitched as each of the bullets tore into it, but did not fall. Silver was useless against it.

"*Your weapon is nothing to me, woman.*" It sounded on the verge of merriment.

Hiram stepped forward, drawing attention to himself. "So

was yours, unless you're expecting us to catch our death of cold."

It smirked, lips twitching beneath the beard. *"Not weapon, man Grange. Summoning."* It pointed up at the cliff, where the river had struck, and Hiram felt the ground shake beneath his feet. The confluence. Something was coming through. Something *vast*.

"Kedra, run!" She was directly below it, and bolted further along the path without looking up, trusting him totally. Hiram limped backwards, unable to take his eyes from the cliff as soil showered down.

The cliff blew open, rock flying outwards into the river, onto the path, and as he raised his good arm to fend off debris, praying nothing large found him, he saw something burst forth, heard it shrieking, saw fire spew, and then dust rolled over him and he saw nothing for long moments. Disorientated, he cowered there, pulling his coat over his mouth so he could breathe, hearing something scream above him as it circled, powerful wings moving the dust around. It was searching for him.

The Grandfather was nothing if not showy. It had summoned a dragon, perhaps inspired by the legends of Krakow's founding. Maybe there was truth to the tales of Krakus defeating the serpent of Wawel Hill, and this was the same one returned from the void. On a confluence, anything was possible, and what the rusalka had begun, the dragon had been called upon to finish. Hiram was flattered, though he knew it was like using a bazooka to kill a cockroach. The beast shrieked again, chilling him more than the river or blizzard had.

If dead cockroaches were what you wanted, a bazooka would do you a hell of a job.

The air cleared, faster than he would have liked. The boulevard was an urban war zone of scattered rock, dirt, and masonry. At the top of the cliff, outhouses still huddled precariously, and Hiram guessed the masonry came from foundations or cellars of some sort. Above it all, circling back for a fresh pass, the dragon of legend, given new half-life. Sixty feet long, it was more skeleton than meat, papyrus-yellow bones protruding from mummified flesh. The wings were cartilage and tatters, beating through habit more than need, for the beast was riding the power of the confluence that birthed it rather than the currents of the storm. Its long skeletal neck craned round, empty eye sockets finding him, and it roared with triumph.

The fury of the sound froze him where he cowered, for he knew death when he heard it. The wheeling dragon was being controlled, and a glance at the Grandfather's straining face told of the effort required to do so. This was no revenge-driven rusalka, needing only a gentle push in Hiram's direction. This was an ancient denizen of the spaces beyond the confluence, and having been freed, it would not willingly return. Hiram would die, probably very soon, and then Krakow would burn, leaving a million charred corpses for the crows. It would be stopped, eventually. One dragon could not take the military might that would be sent forth, once the politicians accepted what was before them, but the lives lost would be unthinkable.

Whether his life was a lie or not, his purpose had not changed. Hiram knew that if he could survive the first pass, he would have a chance to stop this. Kedra was gone. Whether she had kept running or lay broken and buried beneath the rubble made no difference. It was up to him, as it should be. He was Hiram Grange, and this is what he did.

The dragon dived towards him. He searched for cover, found none, and stumbled towards the river. Clutching his agonised arm, he leaned forward, letting gravity help him. The dragon drew breath, and he knew he was going to be too late.

Its wizened chest contracted, and flames billowed from its bony maw, an impossible furnace rushing to meet him, the roar pounding his ears, and he screamed as he pushed forward one more time. Dragon breath met him as his foot touched the river bank, a moment of staggering heat and pain, then he had fallen through, into the Vistula, the ice water giving instant relief. Only the speed of the creature's flight saved him, for it was moving too fast to turn and boil the river around him, its fires instead raking the boulevard where he had been.

Surfacing, he floundered for the bank, pulling himself out as he counted the seconds, his skin blistering. Around him, trees were burning. Snow still fell, but less densely now, the heat from the rubble and pavement melting the flakes before they could land. The dragon had passed over the hill, was out of sight, but he didn't have long. Under the wodnik's control, it would be turning tightly, rushing back. The wodnik still stood on the surface of the river, beside the path along the shore, body tense and unmoving as it battled wills with the ancient force it had enslaved.

Hiram limped towards it, eyes on his own feet, shutting down the pain, putting it aside for later. His first steps were slow, but with a roar that emptied his lungs, he pushed them to move faster. The wodnik did not flinch as he approached, a water god in its domain, knowing Hiram had nothing with which to harm it, but its eyes widened as he dropped to his knees, clasping his hands imploringly. "Stop this! Put the beast back where it belongs! I'll come with you, whatever you want, just spare this place!"

Its eyes flickered with dead amusement, and it snickered. *"Refuse the gifts he gives me? Never, man Grange. You die, and he gives me more toys.*" It struggled to control its new pet, such a summoning beyond its usual grasp. The man in white had stoked the confluence. The army of rusalka, and the dragon whose wings he heard approaching, had landed at this thing's feet, presents with which to terminate the man Grange and his pretty companion. At the feet of the Polish god, Hiram started to sob.

"Please … the people … the little children …"

The wodnik chuckled, leaned closer. "*No, little man.*"

Hiram looked up, eyes dry. "Can't say I didn't offer," he said. Grabbing the slime-ridden beard in his good left hand, he rocked back onto his feet and yanked hard. It shrieked as it stumbled forward, shrieked again when it realised it was out of the water. Echoing the cry, drowning it out, the dragon filled the night with fury, suddenly free of the Grandfather's influence.

Hiram yanked again, dragging the frantic god further onto the shore. "Thought so. Away from the water, you're nothing." The dragon shot overhead, roaring. "Do you think it might be a forgive-and-forget sort of a dragon? Or is it the other kind, that hunts down little gods who fuck with it, and finds out what temperature immortal flesh cooks at?" In the water the wodnik was untouchable, master of its dominion. If Hiram had not surprised it, he did not think any force on earth could have forced it onto land if it did not want to go. Now it was no stronger than the ancient body it presented to the world, and even crippled as he was, Hiram threw it easily, sending it sprawling at the foot of the dragon statue. The fires had licked the metal, and he felt the warmth from it as he pulled a set of handcuffs, lined with pink fur, from his coat. "Normally, these are for personal use," he said, binding the wodnik to the statue's leg, talking to stop himself from losing concentration. *There's still the dragon*, he reminded himself. *I have to put the dragon back in the confluence.* While it would no longer target him specifically, freed of the wodnik's control it would rampage.

"*Man Grange, release me. I share much with you, share so good with you.*"

"Part ownership in a filthy Polish river? Some sort of timeshare arrangement? Thank you, no. Now. Hold still." Drawing his Webley left-handed, he placed the barrel to the wodnik's forehead. "Say cheese." The shot slammed the creature back against the metal, but the wound was already healing when Hiram leaned in to look. Iron didn't work, either. "Well, it was worth a try. Now be quiet. There's a dragon looking for you, remember?" The Grandfather didn't answer, and the hatred in its eyes gave Hiram a boost of immense satisfaction.

Far above them, the clouds lit up, the dragon blowing off steam as it circled. Head tilted back to watch for it, snow melting on his cheeks, Hiram reloaded the Webley and judged the distance to the hole the dragon's emergence had smashed in the cliff. It wasn't far at all, barely twenty feet. Another day, he could have been inside in moments. Pocketing his gun, he found purchase on the cliff face behind the statue, leaving the cowering wodnik behind, and began to climb one-handed. The going was tough, but desperation made him scramble faster than he had hoped.

It was instinct that made him believe the dragon would seek revenge on the Grandfather, and he hoped for Krakow's sake that it wasn't just wishful thinking. His plan was simple. Let the dragon finish the wodnik for him. Draw its attention. Lead it into the cave. Make it follow him into the confluence at the heart of the hill. Hope it could not simply turn around and fly back out.

Of course, he wouldn't care by that last point. He would be dead, or mad, or possibly both. As far as he knew, and he appreciated now how little he had always known, no human had ever emerged from a confluence before, alive or dead. Some had gone in, or so the dissembling Bothwell would have it, but they were never seen again.

Hauling himself over the jagged lip, he saw that it was not so much a tunnel, but more a rip in the hill's heart, sharp and uneven, pitch-black except for a blush of strange colour deep inside. The light, the confluence, was impossible to focus on, and trying made him nauseous and cold. It would tear his soul open to bathe in that light, he knew, but wasn't that what he had craved since seeing a pale reflection of it, many years ago? That it would drive him to grieving tears of joy and lunacy to take even a few steps closer was a given, yet he wanted to, intended to. To draw the beast back down this rabbit hole, he needed to check the lie of the land, didn't he? Yes, that was the reason for him to creep further in. That would do nicely. He stepped forward.

A thump behind him shook the hill and made him stumble backwards, almost throwing him out. Snapped from his fugue, he turned away from the light. Soon he would know it fully. Earlier he had mused on whether he had the strength to do as Kedra had, to stand and fight in the face of his world shredding around him, and now he knew he did not. He would leave this reality, rather than try to understand its rewritten rules. If he could take the dragon with him, save Krakow, then the sacrifice pleased him. It would not be an act of cowardice, done in that way. It would be martyrdom at its most magnificent, and while nobody else would know what he had done, he would plunge more surely for telling himself that lie. Perhaps Kedra would even forgive him.

The dragon stood on the boulevard, dripping with melted ice and snow, back legs steaming in the river. Its old bones gleamed like plague as it lowered its head to the cowering wodnik. Unable to see the confrontation without hanging out of the cave, Hiram examined the dragon's massive head, just feet away from him, looking for weak spots. There were none that he could see, and he gripped the Webley, thinking of his dead mother, his long-absent father. Maybe they were waiting for him somewhere behind that light. If that were the case he could look forward to levelling some of his love and hate, in equal measure, at them.

The Grandfather babbled in Polish, plaintive and pathetic. The dragon cocked its head, bones creaking against one another, and drew a breath. Fire spewed from its maw, smashing over the wodnik, hitting the base of the cliff and billowing up. Hiram threw himself backwards, landing on his shattered arm with a cry, black dots splashing in front of his eyes. He fought to stay conscious as furnace-heat licked over him. The onslaught lasted longer than he thought he could bear, cooking the air around him so that he held his breath rather than take another scalding lungful.

When the roar and crackle stopped, he rose, gasping, eyes streaming in the heat. The lower edge of the cave's opening glowed with faint red fury, the sharp edges smoothed by the inferno, and he couldn't get close enough to look down at whatever remained of the Grandfather. The dragon paused, examining its work, then lifted its head to the skies, great wings extending.

Hiram levelled the Webley and bade farewell to life. All he had to do was draw its attention, make it chase him down

rather than incinerate him where he stood. He was ready. The pain wracking him, making him old and slow, would be gone soon. He would be able to conquer it, for the minutes it took to reach the confluence.

As he cocked the gun, drawing a sharp breath as the numb, blistered skin of his hand stretched, the dragon paused, aware of something new. Hiram's finger tensed as he drew aim on the hollow socket of its right eye.

Kedra dropped from somewhere above the cave entrance, feet first, her poise a thing of poetry, and landed on the creature's brow. Her knees absorbed the impact of landing, and she rolled over her left shoulder, sliding only inches before stopping in a graceful crouch at the back of the skull. Turning, she caught Hiram's eye once before throwing herself flat, wedging her body between ridges of bone as the monster threw back its head and roared irritation at the clouds.

Hiram stepped forward, trying to draw her attention, but the heat from the molten edge of the cave was too great, and he was beaten back. "Kedra! I have it! Get off, woman!"

The dragon quietened, and he heard her call back. "*Nie.* You know what must be done to send this back. Is my city. My choice."

"No! Kedra, I'm ready! Let me do this!"

"Cannot … you are the one. You are …" With a sweep of wings that drove the heat back towards him, the dragon took to the skies with a muscular surge, out of his view above the cave, and he could not tell whether her last word really had been *chosen.* Stunned, he waited, hearing the dragon's cries, unable to see what was happening, not knowing what Kedra hoped to achieve. While he heard gunshots, they would be nothing more than an irritant to a creature that size, even if it proved vulnerable to her silver-laced payload. All she could do was piss it off.

They appeared over the river, dancing through the snow, and he could not see whether Kedra was still clinging to its head, though he assumed she must be, given its erratic progress. There was a distant gunshot, and the dragon wheeled back towards the cave. As it drew nearer, he saw her eyeing the opening in the cliff, her gun drawn. The dragon started to pull up, and she jammed the barrel against a ridge of forehead and pulled the trigger. It flinched, angling back down towards him. She was using the weapon like a cattle prod, herding the monster home.

Looking up, she saw him still there, waved him frantically aside. Hiram came to his senses, shoving himself into a shallow hollow in the wall as the dragon shafted into the cave, filling it as it wriggled home. He heard two more shots, and then it was past. Stepping out, he saw the beast framed in those sickening colours, Kedra silhouetted atop its head, and he wanted to chase them down, drag her free, but the colours speared him and he dropped to his knees, vomiting blood onto the cave floor as they vanished in an explosion of light.

Wawel Hill shook as the confluence digested them, and rubble began to fall from the tunnel's ceiling in crushing chunks. Steadying himself, instinct his master, Hiram staggered to the entrance of the cave, ignoring the oven heat. Throwing himself into the snowy night, the cave collapsing behind him, he smashed once into the cliff on the way down, then smacked into the boulevard in a crumpled heap.

Finally, blessedly, unconsciousness swept him in its maw, and he welcomed it.

"It has been a week."

"Yes."

"There is no word?"

"None. But no body, no sign of Kedra, nothing but rubble for the world's press to speculate on."

"Then you have failed."

"I deny it. He might have killed her, as we planned. The wodnik is gone. I suspect this is his doing."

"Good. Something is salvaged. The creature was becoming demanding. I no longer need deal with it. But this is not evidence of your favourite's survival."

"But …"

"Kedra may have dispatched it. Or Kedra and Grange together."

"You don't know that."

"Neither do you, and it has been a week. I issued fair warning. Your usefulness has ended."

"Please …"

"Do not beg. Your last shallow breaths are worth more. Savour them. Now kneel, woman."

"Wait. My phone."

"And who would be calling a dried-up hag such as yourself? Loved ones? I think not."

"May I find out?"

"Do not linger. I am listening."
"Hello? Hello? Who is this?"

"Who is this?"

Hiram took a deep, silent breath. Kedra's memory sat at his shoulder, his mother and Sadie not far behind, and he gritted his teeth. "It's me."

"Hiram! Thank goodness, Hiram, you have no idea how good it is to hear your voice." Bothwell sounded on the verge of tears, and deep down, his doubts stirred once more.

"You missed me?"

"I've been going out of my mind!" Could she be as clueless as he once had about the masters who controlled her, the work she did? *"Where on earth are you?"*

This was it, his last chance to vanish, and rebirth himself away from the betrayals and lies. He forsook it knowingly. "Warsaw. Krakow was unwelcoming. You've seen the news?" Of course she had, but he needed to ask stupid questions to lull her, regain her trust.

"Between the media panicking about a terrorist attack, and the government denying it, you've fixed the eyes of the world on that city."

"My famed subtlety at play."

"Indeed. Were … were you successful?"

"The rusalka you wanted, that called itself Kedra, is gone."

"*How?*"

"I sent it screaming back into the confluence." Not screaming, not Kedra. Her passing had been magnificent. "It wasn't alone. A spirit thing called a wodnik was controlling it. And there was a dragon."

She paused. "*Dealt with?*"

"Of course. I sent the dragon after Kedra. The wodnik is neutralised." When he came to, moments after greying out, he had seen the sealed entrance to the cave, known there was no chance of going in after Kedra. Dragging the charred carcass of the wodnik from the molten slag that had once been a dragon sculpture, he had stolen a car, driven it outside the city limits. In a desolate field far from the river, he had strained his aching frame to dig a grave. One-handed, he had rolled the wodnik in, and buried it alive. As he filled in the hole, its eyes had opened, shooting hate and fear at him, and he had drawn strength from its helplessness.

"*Good. That's ... excellent, Hiram.*" He could hear the subtext, the unspoken questions she did not dare ask. "*Are there ... loose ends we need to deal with?*"

"We?"

"*You and I.*" She had paused before answering, for a fraction of a second, but it was enough to confirm that she was deep in the fold of the enemy, and he closed his eyes in sorrow. He would have wished otherwise.

"Not that I know of." An army of rusalka roaming the Polish streets? Free of the wodnik's control they would appease their nature, hunting down killers and rapists. Kedra would have found that acceptable.

"*Good. Can you get to an airport?*"

"I'm at the Frederic Chopin right now. My passport is gone."

"I'll send somebody. Just stay where you are, and they'll find you."

"I'll need a doctor when I get back. I'm … a little tender."

"It will be arranged. Hiram … you could have called in sooner."

Hiram smiled, his excuses ready … and partly true. "There are many fine bars in Warsaw."

"Oh, Hiram … a week?"

"I had a great deal of relaxing to do."

"Just this once, I forgive you. It's … it's good to hear your voice, Hiram." She sounded completely genuine. *"Stay where you are. I'll bring you home."*

Hiram hung up, running the fingers of his left hand along his nose, doubting his choices but committing to them nonetheless. The airport thronged around him, humanity surging there and back again, and he limped to a spare bench.

Had he convinced her that he was the old Hiram, true to her cause? He would find out soon enough. Either he would be welcomed back, or executed where he stood. Kedra's mistake had been to announce her suspicions. By going rogue, putting herself outside the circle, she had made herself a target, hampered her access. Hiram would not repeat the error. Keep your friends close, and your enemies closer, wasn't that how the saying went? Hiram's friends, if they had ever been such, were dead. All he had were enemies, and he would hold them very close indeed.

The boy sitting opposite him was reading a polish film magazine. On the cover, his Jodie posed, elegant and intense. Kedra had once reminded him of Jodie. Now Jodie reminded him of Kedra, the woman who had died because she believed he had been chosen, the woman who might have been the dark mirror of his heart. A spear of pain and loss went through him.

Home. Bothwell was bringing him home, that he could tear down the walls from within. Somewhere a man in white plotted and prepared, believing absolute power to be his by right.

Hiram would find that man, and there would be … a conversation.

The Webley sat in his pocket, the sixth chamber unused through all his years of unknowing servitude to that man. Hiram thought he may have finally found a suitable use for it.

His mother, he hoped, would be pleased.

Presenting Chapter One of a new serialized novel

CRAVEN PLACE

BY
RICHARD WRIGHT

C raven Place vomited Tanith through the front door. She tumbled into the morning greys, the wind catching her long black skirt and wrapping it tight around her legs. Her hair, beneath the same gale's enthusiastic encouragement, became a wild and happy beast, half-blinding her as she fought to escape. With the expulsion of each breath she expected red mist to billow out from between her lips, so sure was she that the pain in her ragged lungs meant that blood was flowing.

One traitor foot caught the other, splashing her hard into the February muds. As quickly as that, she was stilled, and the adrenaline that had rushed her along diluted in her veins. To stay there, the wind a violent lover on her back, the slush soaking into her chest, would be a blessed relief.

But time was passing, and they were coming.

Please, she thought, *let me live*. Sobbing with desperation, muscles quivering, she forced herself up from the filth, and on. Fighting the storm, which insisted that the aluminium cattle gate she struggled against must remain closed, she heaved her way onto the fields. The footing was treacherous; arable land gone bad, untended and rebellious. It shifted beneath her steps, making her flight clumsy, draining critical strength from her legs. Behind her, the front door banged furiously, an ironic applause that she had made it so far.

She was not expected to get much further. There was no escaping the witch. Morgan was strong, and the light no longer caused her to beat so hasty a retreat as once it had. Tanith tried to forget the cause of that strength, the lives she had failed to save. Tears sprang to her eyes as she sprinted, dried instantly by the rushing air.

Even in her terror, she slowed as she reached the bottom of the field. The scarecrow was conspicuous through absence, bloating recent memories that made her skin rise up in countless peaks and valleys. No time to remember. No time to dwell. Time only to run, and pray for strength and guidance.

Behind her, Craven Place was now a cancer shape in the background, rough around the edges, crumbling slightly beneath the weight of time. Tanith didn't need to look with her eyes to know that the threat continued. Intuition, and more specialist senses sharpened over years, told her that it was tracking her flight, and knew where to send its mistress when she came hunting.

Climbing the low wall framing the field, she approached the copse, realising too late her mistake in choosing this direction. Morgan had every bit as much power in Hag's Nook as Craven Place itself, perhaps even more. Too late to back away. She would go through, and on. Salvation would, must, lie on the far side. Her heart dancing a percussion on her ribs, she launched herself against tight-knit branches, bearing the scrapes and cuts, blinded by the twigs that whipped her face. On and through. Erupting from foliage, she found her balance before gravity could claim her again. Across the ground the ashes of the witch-fire still clung to stubborn earth, refusing to be snatched up by the winter storm. The morning birds refused to cluster for shelter here. Potent hate seeded the clearing, the copse's black heart, with choking potency. She froze, brief clarity illuminating the scale of her error. The lower creatures knew well enough to give it wide berth, yet here she was, standing at a focal point of Morgan's power. Was she out of her mind?

Tired of watching and waiting, the trees about her leered in, skeletal, charcoal scratches against the reluctant morning light. Tanith felt their attention in her bones, retched at the malignant intensity with which she was scrutinised. She trembled at the power being directed at her.

She was discovered. Intangible fingers caressed her mind, cold and irrefutable. She couldn't move, her limbs no longer willing to journey at her command. They listened to another mistress now.

The world pirouetted, the trees now dark figures dancing a dawn celebration at her capture. Sighing a mocking gale-song, they lulled her through the fear she felt, encouraging the gentle sleep she longed for. Tanith fought with all the gifts she had been given, but her power was insufficient, her mental defences unprepared for the crippling weight of the witch. Fresh tears sprang to her eyes. The sustenance Morgan had drawn to wield this power came from those that Tanith had been unable to protect. Her own failures were being used against her, and despair made it harder to keep fighting.

Sleep, came the coaxing. *Time has passed. We are here. Sleep. To struggle is to feel pain. To know failure. To live misery. So sleep.*

There was no blocking the voice that was not a voice. Tanith tried to hold truths close to her heart. To know failure is to make success sweet. To live misery is to emerge into joy. But what success was worth a failure that took the lives of those in her care? What joy could erase the misery she had allowed to befall unto others?

None. Sleep.

Tanith's exhausted body folded in the wind, slapping rudely against the ground. She did not notice. She had lost her battle, and the witch would soon be upon her.

The cold sun tore apart the clouds. The storm collapsed as abruptly as it had begun. In the undergrowth, nervous birds began a tentative dawn song.

Tanith awoke to light. The trees were dormant once more, and the clearing bathed in mid-morning sun. Two feet from her head, a starling scoured the weed-ridden ground for post-storm pickings. She sat up, wondering, then regretted the sudden movement as the clearing flipped over. When it settled again, liking its new orientation better, Tanith tried to make sense of her unlikely survival.

Hands to her head, she sought a picture of what had happened after she was put under. She should be dead, an eternal servant of one who had taken much from her already, yet she still breathed of her own volition. Why? The clearing had claimed her. The witch had been summoned. She had been defenceless.

Sunlight brushed warmth over her damp skin, and she understood. She had outlasted the storm. The morning had cast it down. Though Morgan could walk in the dim greys of dawn, manifesting beneath true sunlight was still beyond her reach. Even now though, Tanith could feel the clearing stir hungrily. It sensed her awakening, and knew frustration. Though she did not feel the threat of the previous night, she was still in peril. If Morgan could not attack her directly, there were more subtle tools at her disposal. The lower beasts, weak of mind, were easily turned to unnatural acts.

She forced her whining muscles to complete what they had started, pushing herself up and preparing to flee. The storm clouds must have taken refuge in her own head, such was the dizzy fog that came with standing. She could not wait for it to pass. This was a second chance she would be unwise to waste. If she passed out again she might not wake until dusk had stolen over North Wales and made Megan strong again.

She might not wake at all.

Disorientated, she turned briefly on the spot, legs aching as she tried to pick out the way she had come into the clearing. The storm had pulled free so much foliage that it had masked any damage her own blundering flight may have caused, obscuring the clues which might help her choose a path away from Craven Place. In the end it was a random decision, and her faltering escape continued.

Pushing through bushes and trees, drained of the urgency that had powered her earlier that morning, the true force of her exhaustion sank into her. Now the whipping twigs caused tears to flow. The grabbing, snagging branches and thorns yanked her hair and clothes, summoning little cries of frustration. Hag's Nook did not want her to leave. *Stay*, it coaxed, *stay until dusk, and meet the hag*. Seconds were long hours on her journey. The copse was barely fifty metres across, yet eternity passed as she struggled on.

Weeping, she continued, and breaking through a final tangle of thorns and weeds, she found the other side of Hag's Nook. She half expected night to have fallen already, yet the morning sun still stroked the winter fields. With a shudder of relief she saw a shape on the horizon, and realised she had found her destination. On the coast road, squat and proud against the water, sat a church.

Without asking permission of her conscious mind, her legs broke into a sprint. She allowed them to, trying to discard the thought that haunted her. Behind Hag's Nook lay Craven Place. Quiet now, it waited.

Soon, she would have to return.

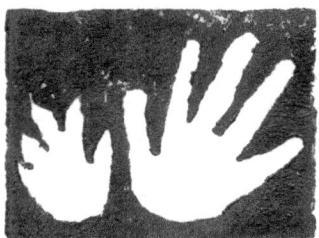

By the time she reached the church, following a grass track running between two fields, her legs felt hollow, but she refused to rest until her task was complete, and she had sought out whatever aid was available.

Approaching the gate to the graveyard, she stumbled again, taking the skin from her knees in landing, but hope energised her, and she scrambled up with hardly a beat missed in her run. The gate was set into a high wall, lending the dead a rare privacy as they rotted. Tanith realised with alarm that she could hear nothing from the other side. It was Sunday morning, surely the busiest day for the sons of Christ?

Slowing, careful that her faltering stride did not drop her again, she rested a hand on the gate. It occurred to her that she was being watched, the notion presenting itself to her awareness as fact. She knew not to discard the feeling. Since childhood, her intuitions had developed into something more, fine-tuning, expanding her awareness of the world around her, and those beyond. On those few occasions when she had ignored her feelings, bad things had happened, no more so than in the last two days. If she felt watched, then there was a watcher. Fear squirted into her stomach.

Pushing hard, she opened the gate. Hinges grated with the wear of weather and abandonment, and she knew it was not in regular use. Tanith stifled her panic. There might be another entrance, better kept, which the flock and shepherds used.

Walking into the overgrown graveyard, she embraced the peace and stillness around her, holding the moment and the relief that came with it. Her body was taut with stress, her skin tight across her face and shoulders. Morgan had been relentless, her assaults exhausting, and she knew that any respite was to be exploited while it lasted. The headstones around her were cracked and crumbled, aged and worn. The church was a square eroded edifice, a squat shape speaking of the practicalities of worship on the Atlantic coast. There was solidity there, comforting and strong. Tanith was certain that evil had never touched this place.

Yet she was being watched. She was sure of it.

There were no signs of life, only ancient death, and her fluttering panic returned. If she could not take help back to Craven Place, then she had damned the souls of those she had already failed. Though she would return herself, she knew now that her power was nothing next to the rise of Morgan's. Her soul would also be stolen, another tool for the witch.

She had to find help.

Breaking into a trot, she approached the alcove entrance to the church. The porch was in the building's shadow, and the space of a second took her from being warmed by the rich golden light of the sun, to being plunged into icy air. Though she knew the chill to be physical rather than spiritual, it felt like an omen.

Hope gone cold.

Her fears proved just. The door was locked. With a sob, she hurled herself against the wood, smacking it with her fists until her arms felt they could no longer swing. The thuds were shallow, the oak of the door deep, but nobody inside could have failed to hear her battering summons. A plaque beside the door confirmed what she had already guessed. The church was no longer in regular use. There was a telephone number through which a caretaker could be contacted, but his was not the spiritual assistance she was so desperate for.

And still, the watcher watched. Now there was true fear to be had in the knowledge, for if there were no holy men to cast curious eyes her way, no churchgoers to stare, then Morgan was the likely agent behind the intense gaze probing across her.

Unwilling to accept that the sanctuary she had hoped for was nothing more than old stone and long-decayed corpses, she ran back out into the graveyard proper.

'Hello?' she called out, staggering into the light. Why would her inner senses have drawn her to the church if there was no aid there? Why would she have felt the compulsion to flee this way? Exhausted, she shuffled past a headstone taller than her own diminutive five foot two, still calling, almost in tears from the sudden, crushing loneliness. '*Hello!*'

'Hello.'

She span at the voice, gasping as the tattered half-man sitting behind the headstone reached up for her.

Craven Place continues in the SHROUD Digital Edition
Read more at www.shroudmagazine.com

RICHARD WRIGHT

RICHARD WRIGHT is an author of strange dark fictions, currently living with his wife and daughter in New Delhi, India. His stories have been widely published in the United Kingdom and USA for over a decade, most recently in magazines and anthologies including *Dark Wisdom*, *Withersin 3.2*, *Beneath the Surface*, *Shroud*, *Tattered Souls*, *Choices*, and the Doctor Who collection *Short Trips: Re:Collections*.

When not tiger hunting or snake wrangling, he wonders what Hiram might make of India, and hopes to one day find out. In the meantime, you can catch up with him on the web at *www. richardwright.org*. Do drop by.

THE SCANDALOUS MISADVENTURES OF

BOOK 1

Jake Burrows

Hiram Grange & the Village of the Damned

Something wicked walks the streets of the picturesque New Hampshire village of Great Bay—something that has inexplicably risen from the grave to wreak a horrifying vengeance.
Only one man can stop it—Hiram Grange—provided he can sober up long enough to answer the call!

BOOK 2

Scott Christian Carr

Hiram Grange & the Twelve Little Hitlers

Hitler has escaped. Twelve of them, to be precise, each cloned from the original, and hiding in the bizarre American underground.
Hiram Grange has been tasked with hunting them down.
The only problem: he's hit rock bottom. His worst binge ever—a mad dance with absinthe, opium and depression …

BOOK 3

Robert Davies

Hiram Grange & the Digital Eucharist

From its global headquarters in Boston, the mysterious Occlusionist Movement is preparing to control the world with its Digital Eucharist, while in the serpentine bowels of the city an ancient demon is unleashed, eager for revenge against the man who imprisoned it years ago—Hiram Grange!

HIRAM GRANGE

BOOK 4

Kevin Lucia

Hiram Grange & the Chosen One

Hiram Grange doesn't believe in fate. He makes his own destiny.
That's a good thing, because Queen Mab of Faerie has foreseen the
destruction of the world, and as usual … it's all Hiram's fault.
He must choose: kill an innocent girl and save the universe …
or rescue her and watch all else burn.
Just another day on the job for Hiram Grange.

BOOK 5

Richard Wright

Hiram Grange & the Nymphs of Krakow

Hiram Grange was already broken when his world was turned
upside down by the horrifying revelations of a beautiful and
dangerous woman. Faced with the possibility that he's been a pawn
in a diabolical game, he seeks the truth in the snows of Krakow.
But the truth is guarded by ancient, winged things,
and the truth has teeth …

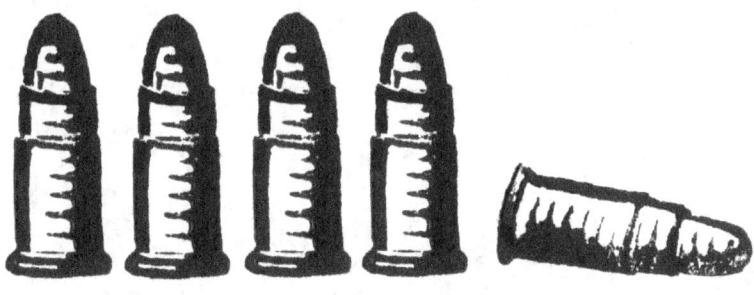

WWW.HIRAMGRANGE.COM

More Great Fiction

Maurice Broaddus
Devil's Marionette

Death comes for the cast and crew of the hit comedy TV Show Chocolate City, impacting not only their personal lives but the prospect of their show's continued success. As each member sinks into their own past, and the spirits of those that came before, the tragedies continue.
When your terror comes to claim you,
who will it be?
Nobody.

R. Scott McCoy
FEAST

Deputy Sheriff Nick Ambrose can look into someone's eyes and glimpse their guilt, to an extent. But when he and his brother take on a psychopathic killer, he gains something more: the ability to see, and devour, souls. Plagued by this terrifying new power, and by the spirits of both his brother and the butcher trapped inside his mind, he sets out to understand and control his new fate and to grapple with the shadowy auras he now sees all around.
Can he command the darkness welling within,
or will he become merely its vessel?

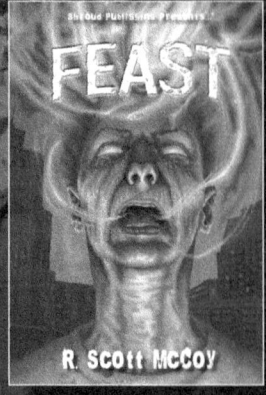

Cindy Little
Intruder

When the powers of an ancient malevolent creature invade a quiet suburban household, a young mother is forced into a pitched battle for the life of her child.
A shocking and intelligent novella from veteran supernatural investigator, Cindy Little.

from Shroud Publishing...

Nathaniel Lambert & Danny Evarts
It's Okay to be a Zombie
**A Full Colour Unchildren's Book
for Anyone with a Dark Side**

Sure, zombies are pretty scary. They stink. They
want to eat your brains. They're terrible house
guests. Who says zombies can't be fun, too?
Don't they look kind of silly falling down and
bumping into things? Sometimes they can even be
cute. So, before you run away screaming for your
lives, stop and appreciate the beauty of the undead.
And remember ...
It's Okay to be a Zombie.

Rio Youers
Mama Fish

At Harlequin High School In 1986, Kelvin Fish
is the oddball, the weird kid that no one will talk to,
except for Patrick Beauchamp, who is determined
to learn more. When Patrick's curiosity leads him
into a bizarre and tragic series of events,
he gets much more than he bargained for.

D. Harlan Wilson
Peckinpah: An Ultraviolent Romance

Life in Dreamfield is a daily harangue of pigs, cornfields,
pigs, fast food joints, pigs, Dollar Stores, pigs, motorcycles,
pigs, and good old-fashioned Amerikan redneckery.
Angry, slick-talking, and ultraviolent to the core, Samson
Thataway and the Fuming Garcias commit art-for-art's-
sake in the form of hideous, unmotivated serial killings.
When an unsuspecting everyman's wife is murdered by the
throng, it is up to Felix Soandso to avenge her death and
return Dreamfield to its natural state of absurdity.

Shroud Anthologies
Dark fiction and horror
in tasty bite-sized pieces

Abominations

17 Spine-tingling Tales of Murderous Monsters
Expertly-crafted, never-before published tales of horrifying
creatures, mythical beasts, and murderous monsters from some
of the best voices in modern horror. With stories from John
Teehan, Anna Lowther, Eric Christ, Rhonda Parrish, William
Vogel, Tracie McBride, Mark Tullius, Kevin Lucia, Brandon
Berntson, Jeff Parish, Lee Zumpe, Lon Prater, Lincoln Crisler,
Gerard Houarner, R. Scott McCoy, Dave Dunwoody, and
Richard Farnsworth. Edited by Timothy Deal.

Beneath the Surface

13 Shocking Tales of Terror
Bram Stoker Award Nominee for Best Anthology of 2008
Supernatural beings, Gothic settings, shadowy creatures, and
atmospheric haunts tantalize and thrill in this collection of
eerie and terrifying old-school works of short fiction. Including
works by Scott Christian Carr, Derek M. Fox, Scott William
Carter, Malon Edwards, Ian Whates, J.T. Glover, Philip
Roberts, Richard Wright, Justin McMahon, Efraim Z. Graves,
Marie Brennan, Angeline Hawkes, and Jake Burrows.

Northern Haunts

100 Terrifying New England Tales
Much more than an anthology, this is an indispensable
guidebook for your journey through the shadowy New
England otherworld. 100 original tales of ghosts, creatures,
mad men, and other horrifying mysteries, each told in the first
person so that the reader can customize these treacherous tales
in order to tantalize friends and terrify family.
Profits from the sale of this book are donated
to the *American Cancer Society*.

www.ingramcontent.com/pod-product-compliance
Lightning Source LLC
Chambersburg PA
CBHW070635130626
46555CB00006B/2550